*For all children who
suffer through war*

**The opinions expressed in this book do not necessarily
reflect the views or policy of UNICEF**

Published by:
The Disinformation Company Ltd.
163 Third Avenue, Suite 108
New York, NY 10003
Tel.: +1.212.691.1605
Fax: +1.212.473.8096

First published in Great Britain by Frances Lincoln Limited.

Library of Congress Control Number: 2003107419

ISBN: 0-9729529-1-8

Printed in Great Britain

Distributed by:
Consortium Book Sales and Distribution
1045 Westgate Drive, Suite 90
St Paul, MN 55114
Toll Free: +1.800.283.3572
Local: +1.651.221.9035
Fax: +1.651.221.0124
www.cbsd.com

Lines
in the
Sand

New Writing on War and Peace

Edited by Mary Hoffman
and Rhiannon Lassiter

**All profits and royalties to UNICEF's
emergency appeal for the children of Iraq**

disinformation

Introduction

You may be studying war at your school and learning about trenches and gas masks. But do you realize how many wars have been going on in the world since the last World War ended in 1945?

In places like Nigeria, Israel, Afghanistan, Kuwait, Kosovo, Rwanda, Vietnam, the Falklands, Iran and Iraq, bombs, bullets and landmines have done their deadly work. But they don't do it on their own; people have to fly the planes, pull the triggers, lay the mines.

You may see the results on the TV news and think it's like the special effects in exciting action films, with explosions and lots of people running. But that blood is real, not the work of make-up artists, and when the people fall down, they don't get up again. They are people like you, who feel pain when they bleed.

The writers and artists who have contributed to this anthology want you to know what has been going on in the world for the last fifty years or so. But they don't want to make you despair about the future of the human race. You, the children of today, are the ones with the power to make it stop. Tomorrow, when you are the grown-ups, you can make the world a more peaceful place.

Mary Hoffman   R Lassiter

Contents

The road to war

The Butcher

As I was out walking one fine summer's morning
I saw a young man shot dead in the street.
A butcher came by in a blood-spattered apron,
crying, "Come and buy my lovely fresh meat!"

A soldier ran up and he stopped by the body.
He spat in its face and his boot cracked its spine.
"You coward, you scumbag, you rat from the shadows –
you'll no longer murder no buddies of mine."

An old man appeared and he knelt by the body.
"I hope God rewards you, young comrade," he said.
"Your life was given in fighting for freedom,
but the cause needs martyrs and I'm glad that you're dead."

A young woman came running and fell on the body.
She howled in anguish. Tears ran down her cheek.
She cried, "Do you love me? Oh why don't you answer?
Do you love me, my darling? Oh why won't you speak?"

A small boy came up then and stared at the body.
"Oh, why do you lie there, your face turned away?
Won't you play with me, Daddy, 'cos I'm so lonely,
and the house is so cold, and the streets are so gray."

Then up stepped the soldier and pointed his sten gun.
"Let that be a lesson," he said to the child.
"You deserve nothing better than to stay in the gutter,
so do what you're told and grow meek and mild."

The old man came forward, courageous as any.
"Don't heed what he says, boy. You listen to me.
Just look at your father and learn this one lesson:
revenge is no sin till your people are free."

The widow sprang forward to cradle her baby.
"They'll poison your mind, son, so pay them no heed.
Look to the future, when you are a father,
with a life to live and a family to feed."

The boy's eyes were misty with tears for his father.
He looked down the street as he held the cold hand.
He glimpsed himself there, crouched in a doorway
with blood in his eyes and a gun in his hand.

And behind him he saw that same butcher come walking,
at home as you please, like he owned the whole street,
wiping his hands on his blood-spattered apron,
crying, "Come and buy my lovely fresh meat!"

Nigel Gray

Lifeblood (Iraq 2003)

They told us the invasion would start soon.

We drilled a well behind our house,
For drinking water, for the siege.
But what we hit was oil.

Dark and rich and glistening it spilled out
from the puncture wound.
We watched it as it oozed and pooled and
    clotted in the dust.
We watched it
And we listened to the skies.

Kate Thompson

Jihad

It is December 1202, and Arthur de Caldicot, now 16, has joined the Fourth Crusade. He is in Zara on the coast of Croatia with many thousands of Crusaders including Lord Stephen de Holt, Milon de Provins and his 13-year-old squire, Bertie.

Is all war unholy?

When armies fight, do they always both claim that God is on their side?

Does Mother Church have to speak with a tongue of fire?

Do innocent and helpless people always get caught up in it?

My eyelids are drooping. Five times I have vomited and my throat's so sore. My head's reeling.

Merlin told me once that if only I could ask the right questions...

From my room in the tower-house, I watched a boat, little larger than our landing-skiff, skimming between us and the island which is called Ugli and looks so pretty. She had two masts, one about twenty-five feet tall and one in the stern much shorter, and she was skipping and bouncing over the waves. The very strong west wind was blowing a gale and pushing her onshore.

The helmsman swung the boat round to face me; she came racing in, and I doubled down the ninety-four steps and ran down to the water to meet her.

The moment she crunched into the gravel, her two sails were like huge white birds struggling in an invisible net; her rigging whipped and cracked; at the top of the mainmast, the little wind-pennant whirred.

There were only seven people aboard. The helmsman and his mate, two bearded men, and three women wearing strange, crimson wimples that reached below their waists, and walnut-colored skirts down to their ankles.

The older man called out to me. I couldn't understand him.

"Greetings in God!" I said, and steadied the bow. The man frowned.

"Do you speak English? Français?"

"Français. Oui, oui."

"Moi aussi. Un peu."

The man shook his head and spoke to his companion. "Allah go with you!" he said.

The same words the dying man in Coucy said, and the traders in Venice. They were Saracens!

The older man disembarked, and the younger one followed him, carrying a long box quite like a coffin. They left the three women to look after themselves, and they all got the bottoms of their skirts wet. They chirruped like springtime finches.

Leaving the helmsman and his mate to haul down the sails, I led the Saracens up to our tower-house, but no one was there, so I took them to Milon's house. Milon had gone off to discuss rules of conduct with Villehardouin, but his priest, Pagan, was in the hall.

So were at least a dozen knights and their squires, and Bertie was still lying in the corner on a heap of straw.

At first, the Saracens thought we were Zarans. The old man looked like thunder and his eyebrows twitched when Pagan told him who we are and how we've recaptured Zara, and are sailing to Jerusalem.

To begin with, though, he was courteous and so was Pagan.

He said his name was Nasir and he was a singing teacher.

"Like Ziryab!" I cried. "I've learned about him."

Nasir stroked his black beard. He told us the young man was his disciple and was called Zangi. He told us the women were his two wives and his daughter.

"Two wives!" I exclaimed.

"The other two are at home," Nasir replied. "Allah has spared them."

Four wives! No English woman would agree to that!

"What are your names?" I asked the women.

"They have names for me," Nasir rasped. "Not for you."

I can hear him now.

"You hypocrites! What do you care about your holy places? You use your tents as churches. All you want is our wealth. Our gold and silks and spices…"

At first, Pagan and Milon's men were patient. They've exchanged insults with Saracens before.

"You're pests!" said Nasir. "Swarms of flies without wings. You infidels! You attack people of your own faith."

Then the Frenchmen started to mutter.

"You're pigs!" said Nasir. "Leprous pigs. The sons of

sows!"

At this, Pagan pointed at the Saracen women. "They've stolen their color from night," he jeered. "They've stolen their breath from old latrines."

"You yellow-faced Christian," Nasir snarled. "The nation of the Cross will fall."

Pagan raised both hands. "In the name of God..." he yelled.

Nasir stood up. He looked like one of the angry Old Testament prophets.

"In the name of Allah!" he retorted, and his voice was trembling. "We have a gift for you."

He stepped over to Zangi, then beckoned the three women. They huddled over the coffin-box. Then there was a clatter and they sprang apart, all five of them brandishing scimitars and howling.

"Allah! Hand of Allah! Allah!" they howled.

Everyone ducked and dived and scrambled. We all drew our short knives.

"Jihad!" roared the singing teacher. "The vengeance of God has come down on you!"

They killed three of us and wounded four more. They tried to cut Bertie in half but Pagan threw himself over his body, and so they killed him instead.

But there were more of us. Milon's knights overpowered Nasir and then Zangi, and slit their throats, and disarmed the women.

The women began to beat their throats and scream.

I couldn't... I couldn't watch any more. Not as the men began to rip off their clothes.

I ran out.

Anywhere.

But there's nowhere. Nowhere in this dark world to hide.

Milon's men slung their five bodies into the salt water.

They won't go away, though... I don't know how to stop myself thinking.

I don't want to talk to Lord Stephen. I want to be alone.

Wounding, killing...

When is it wrong and can it ever be right?

Poor Stupid. The boy in the mangonel. Giscard. The Zaran councillors whose heads were cut off. Rampaging Frenchmen and Venetians. That man, the one I wounded. Nasir and Zangi and the women with no names. Pagan. Milon's men. All the knights in my seeing stone.

What am I to do when I cannot even tell who is innocent and helpless, and who is not?

Women killers!

How deeply the Saracens hate us.

All this hatred and suffering. How can one person make any difference at all?

This chapter is taken from King of the Middle March, *the third part of Kevin Crossley-Holland's Arthur trilogy.*

Kevin Crossley-Holland

Counting

When they do war
They forget how to count

They forget how to count
And that's how they do it.

They come
They kill

They kill
They go

They give us
No numbers
No names
They disappear them
They vanish them
It's how they do it.

They come
They kill

They kill
They go

Names are deleted
Numbers are un-counted
Bodies are un-included
Faces are un-remembered
That's how they do it.

They come in
They flush out

They mop up
They take out

No numbers
No names

No names
No numbers

And it's worth it,
they say.
It's worth it.
Believe us, it's worth it
believe us.
Oh yes it IS worth it
if you forget how to count.
It IS worth it
if you forget the numbers.
It IS worth it
if you forget the names.
It IS worth it
if you forget the faces.
That's how they do it.

But
we're counting.
Watch us:
we're counting.
Listen:
we're counting.
And –

– we count.

Michael Rosen

This poem is dedicated to all the dead of all wars who are not counted.

I can remember when the Vietnam war was going on, we never found out how many Vietnamese died. In the war against Afghanistan, which we were told was "worth it," we never found out how many our leaders killed. There was every chance that as many innocent people died in that war as were killed in the twin towers. Now, after the war in Iraq, we may never find out how many Iraqis have died.

Stop

In a room somewhere there's a man at the top
and he's spent all our money at the weapons shop.
He's explaining to the army where the bombs should drop
and he doesn't want to hear when we tell him to stop.

In a faraway city when the soldiers come
and the bombs dive in with a whistle and a hum
and the children scream and the children run
the peace is lost and the damage done.

In a distant place where the bullets fly
and the great green tanks go rolling by
the dogs all howl and the orphans cry
when death drops down from a deep-blue sky.

In a broken land there's a bombed-out street
where the people of the village used to meet
where the children played in the desert heat
and the haunting silence is complete.

Jacqui Shapiro

The Peace Weavers

Hilde Browne hates living with her American father Frank, on a military base in Suffolk, England. Her brother Tom is happy but she'd rather live with their mother Maeve. Inspired by the discovery of an Anglo-Saxon peace weaver on an archaeological dig, Hilde wants to weave peace too, but it's early 2003 and war with Iraq looks inevitable. How can she or anyone stop the war? During a meal with the van Jennions family – Lieutenant Karl, his wife Marty and three children Friedman, Olivia and Cally – Hilde has an idea.

"**N**ow if you'll link hands," Marty stood at the end of the table. "Karl will say grace." Hilde felt Olivia's hot little hand trying to hold hers. The touch of Friedman's fingers sent charges up her arm.

"It's my bit of peace-weaving I suppose," said Marty, as if she'd noticed Hilde's awkwardness, and they all sat down. "Don't you just love that concept? I think it makes for more peaceful meal-times anyhow. Now Hilde, what will you have? It's Boston Baked Beans from the Moosewood Cook Book."

Hilde stammered a reply, and nearly dropped the plate Marty handed her. Her right arm was still tingling. But it wasn't as if all this religious stuff was new. Maeve had friends who did it, but – BUT – she hit upon the difference – her mother's friends lived their religion, were pacifists most of them. It was the hypocrisy of Bomber van Jennions invoking God that was making her feel ill. And now she noticed a cross-stitched "Blessed are the Peace Makers" on the wall opposite, above Frank's head, next to photographs of men in uniform. The family had obviously been in the US military for generations.

"Several of my mother's friends," she found her voice at last. "In the Peace Movement – they do it – link hands – say grace – all that stuff – but they try to live – enact their beliefs."

Frank's mouth fell open. Tom stared at his plate wishing he wasn't there. Marty was a ladle-bearing statue.

"What's the Peas Movement?" said Olivia and Cally together.

Hilde pushed beans round her plate as Lieutenant van Jennions explained that some people believed that you should never take up arms even if another country invaded yours. "They believe that when someone hits your cheek, you should offer them the other one."

"Isn't that what it says in the Bible?" said Olivia.

"It's an active thing. Pacifism isn't p-a-ss-i-v-ism." Hilde spelled it out.

Friedman burned with admiration. Hilde had voiced thoughts he hadn't realized he had. She'd opened his eyes, his mind, his heart to what was important. He'd been wrong about her character. She had a stunning character. She was brave, outspoken, magnificent! No wonder the touch of her fingers made his blood fizz.

27

"How do you square doing what you do with being a Christian, Pop?"

Karl van Jennions sounded slightly impatient, as if the answer was obvious. "Well son, the trouble with turning the other cheek is that the guy hits that too, and probably someone else's as well. You've surely heard of the concept of the Just War? War's evil, but sometimes it's one's duty to go to war to prevent a greater evil. Like in 1939 to stop Hitler, and in '91 to stop Saddam Hussein when he invaded Kuwait. The USA is a big powerful country and it's our duty to go to the aid of smaller countries."

"Like Superman?" said Olivia.

"A bit like Superman." Her father tugged one of her pigtails. "And that's why I'll be flying off again soon to keep an eye on Saddam." He turned to Friedman. "I hope that's answered your question, son."

Hilde's head was a jumble of counter-arguments. Oil came into it somewhere. That was it – the good old USA didn't go round defending all the little countries that needed help, only countries with oil they needed for their oversized cars. And the F15s weren't just keeping an eye on Saddam. Things had moved on. Now there was talk of "liberating" Iraq. For liberate, read invade. Bomb enough people and you might hit Saddam. She glanced at Friedman who was regarding his father thoughtfully, and then at her brother who had recovered from his embarrassment.

"What exactly do you do, Lieutenant, when you fly

over Iraq?" Tom felt he should give the guy a chance to put the record straight. "I mean, some people say you're already bombing the Iraqi people." Maeve and Hilde for instance.

"Well, no Tom, we're not. We're making sure Saddam's forces stay put, and we're keeping a look-out for Weapons of Mass Destruction."

"And if you find any?" said Hilde.

"We have taken some out."

"Is that why the inspectors can't find any?"

"Do you ever get shot at?" Tom knew where Hilde's questions were leading.

The Lieutenant hesitated as Marty told Olivia and Cally they could leave the table if they wished and come back later for dessert. Then he turned back to Tom.

"Let's say we're pretty good at looking after ourselves, and I should say I see myself as a peace-keeper not a war-monger. No soldier, 'specially not one who has seen action, likes war. In fact," he looked straight at Hilde, "you could say I'm one of your peace weavers too, but I weave in and out of the clouds, dodging fire from Saddam's anti-aircraft guns, looking for WMDs."

That was obscene.

Frank chipped in, "If you want peace, prepare for war, as the Romans said."

"Exactly," said Karl.

"NO!" cried Hilde. "If you want peace, prepare

for peace, weave peace! Talk! Word weave! Spend money helping poor countries. Attack war and the causes of war!"

Suddenly it became clear to her what a 21st Century peace weaver must do — weave a web, a world-wide web. Mobilize. She got up, couldn't wait to get onto a computer and email everyone she knew. She would organize the biggest anti-war petition ever, the biggest demonstrations that the world had ever seen. The streets would be full, offices, factories and classrooms empty. Public opinion would STOP THE WAR!

Julia Jarman

The Apple's Story

It might have been the apple
My enemy was aiming at,
I like to think it was
And no doubt my enemy
Would like to think the same,
For in later life such a thought
Would have saved him much guilt.
Whatever,
I was about to eat the apple,
There it was, up against my teeth
When his bullet smashed straight through it.
A perfect shot.
The apple exploded,
And an apple seed lodged in my skull
Somewhere between the left eye socket
And the top of the cranium.
Due to the richness of the soil
By the following spring
A seedling apple-tree had sprouted.

And thirty years later,
Another war and another soldier came by,
And he plucked an apple from the tree that I had become,
And I whispered,
"Be aware, be aware!"
But he mistook my voice for the wind rattling
The tree's wet leaves,
And as he raised the fruit to his mouth
Once more it looked too good a target to ignore,
And once more it exploded in a shower
Of juice and blood and bones.
Ever since Adam
People have been aiming at apples,
And only at apples,
And at nothing but apples,
And there is an orchard that stretches
To the far ends of the earth
With blossom that smells of cordite,
With fruit that tastes of loss.

Brian Patten

The Invitation

no time to ask, no time to question,
fulfilling our task will teach them a lesson,
expectations are high, morale is low,
the hour is nigh and over we go.

something to drink, a bite to eat,
my heart disappears down into my feet,
as for the bombs – when they stop we'll all know
it's time for our helmets and over we go.

what should i do and what should i be?
when i look at this view, what is it i see?
on bended knee, pray god's mercy show,
i count to three, and then over we go.

Robin Grey

It Won't Be Long Now

The following piece refers to the Jacobite sieges of Edinburgh Castle and Stirling Castle in 1745–46, when the forces of the "Young Pretender," Prince Charles Edward Stuart ("Bonnie Prince Charlie") opposed British troops loyal to King George I. Names and dates don't matter, though: the civil strife the conflict caused is universal.

I t won't be long now.

Soon the first chill light of the January dawn will cut across the rocky outcrop of the Castle Rock, crisp and clear upon the ice. Not long now until he'll be relieved, allowed the meager comfort of a soldier's cot, and some other poor soul takes the Watch. He rubs his hands, feeling the bones crack, and the dull nagging pain of new feeling as blood courses once more into the numbed flesh of his fingers.

No change.

Nothing to report.

Not even the most black-hearted fool would venture out on a night like this. He clutches his rifle to his breast, hard and tight, its familiar form a cold comfort against whatever the coming dawn might bring.

It won't be long now until they feel its fire.

He wraps his brother's greatcoat tight about him. His coat now, since that other fortress siege, that other Castle Rock. His, since a musket-shot lodged in his brother's gut. He sniffs the coarse wool of the collar scratching against his face. It still carries his brother's scent. Whiskey. Tobacco. Even now.

Three months had passed since he had sat with him in the cellars beneath the huddled rash of tumbledown tenements, spreading down from the towered ridge of the capital. His kinsman had laughed in wonder at these marvels as they marched behind their prince through the cobbled causeways of the Old Town. The buildings – row upon row of great wooden giants, looming six, seven, eight stories high – amazed the country boy. He had never seen such a place as this. And the people – twenty thousand souls crammed together within the city walls – cheering, roaring out a hero's welcome. A hundred faces loomed out from every door and alley.

Fit for a king, it was. Their king. No other.

The crowd were fickle. That's what Uncle had said before they left their home in the high country. He had served under the prince's father, thirty years past. "Watch the tooth behind the smile, lad," the old man had warned. "It'll bite harder and cut deeper than any soldier's blade."

His brother had laughed in his face. Uncle had grown bitter in his dotage, he said. He had lost his lands and livelihood as punishment for fellowship with the old king, and, his sword broken, had lacked the will or wit to forge it anew in the fire of battle. Where his sire had stumbled, the prince would stride through this land. His land. His, by right of birth and blood. The usurper's men might be the finest soldiers in the world, but they fought for silver coin. They fought because the king – their king, not ours – bid them do so. We fought for honor. For tradition, too. The prince might not match them, at first, in arms or numbers, but it was God's will that he should prevail, that his house and his faith should endure.

"It won't be long now!" his brother had beamed. "With God's will it won't be long now before our people welcome our prince – their prince – to his throne."

He had felt his skin tingle, then, touched by the fire of his brother's words. He had been warmed, too, by the welcome they had received as they marched through the gates of the capital. They were heroes.

But few of those that cheered their way through those gates had chosen to take up arms for the prince. As conflict with the castle garrison grew near, the smiles of welcome had turned quickly to suspicious scowls, and to something more. Was it fear he saw in those tired eyes as he scurried alongside his kinsmen? Thousands seemed to pass them as they made their way up through the steep warren of alleyways leading to the promontory of the Castle Rock. Thousands, fleeing their homes in readiness for the battle they knew was soon to come, retreating to a safe distance, far from the range of the castle guns. Was it bitter tight-lipped hate he saw in their eyes? He wanted to stop each and every one and shout in their stupid faces, "It's for you! It's all for you! We're heroes, don't you see?"

At noon enemy cannons thundered from the castle walls. Their artillery lashed out, bringing the timbers of the rebels' tenement hideaways down upon their heads, turning their time-weathered walls to dust.

Within the hour it was done.

For four hours he sat with his brother, huddled in the cellars beneath the blasted homesteads, watching as his kinsman's life leaked slowly away. Faithfully he promised his kin that all would be well: that their cause was just, that it was God's will that the prince should prevail.

"It won't be long now!"

As darkness fell he brushed away his tears, took up his brother's rifle, slipped his arms into the blood-dampened sleeves of a heavy coarse-haired greatcoat too large for him by far. No matter. He'd been only ten years on this earth, and was small for his age – or so his brother had teased. With God's will there would be time enough for him to grow into it.

He left his hiding place – left his brother in the rubble of the past. The townsfolk were returning, tearfully inspecting the shattered remnants of their homes. They glowered at him as he passed through the ruins. "Fools," he thought, "selfish fools to prize their homes higher than their honor."

Now. Three months had come and gone since then.

A cruel winter was upon them. Finding little welcome left in the capital, the prince had turned his attentions northwards, upon another favored seat of his forefathers. Another prize to be won for honor and for faith. And for blood.

Here they were not met with smiles and open arms, but entered anyway. And here they'd stay until their prince reclaimed his birthright, or his cause was lost forever upon the blood of the battlefield.

Either way – God's will or not – it wouldn't be long now.

David Kinnaird

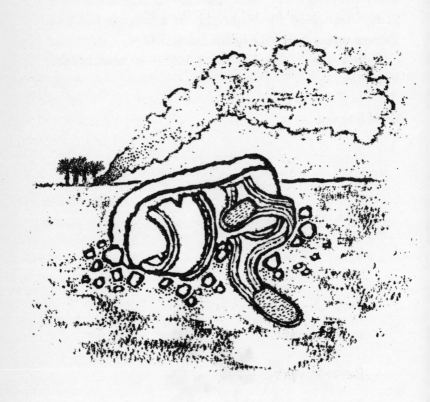

A Small Disaster

They said on the early morning news

It was a small disaster.

Ten were killed, five of them children

In the blue Toyota,

A family fleeing from the fighting.

It is the fog of war, the Colonel said.

It is nobody's fault. The men get jittery.

I told them to stop, the soldier said,

But they just kept coming.

Soon they will be laying out all the small disasters

End to end in children's coffins.

Look! they stretch across the desert to the sea.

Joanna Troughton

During A War

Best wishes to you & yours,
he closes the letter.

For a moment I can't
fold it up again –
where does "yours" end?

Dark eyes pleading
what could we have done
differently?

Your family,
your community,
circle of earth, we did not want,
we tried to stop,

we were not heard
by dark eyes who are dying
now. How easily they
would have welcomed us in
for coffee, serving it
in a simple room
with a glorious rug.

Your friends & mine.

Naomi Shihab Nye

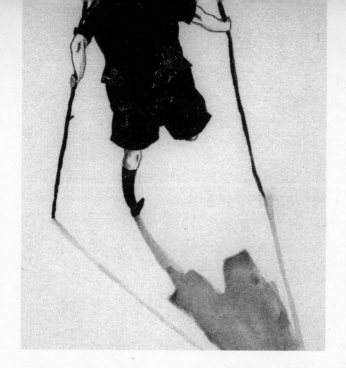

Hidden Danger

This land was our land, this land was yours and mine
Passed to sons and daughters, down the family line.
A place to plant, a place to grow, a place where cattle grazed
But Mother Nature's land has now cruelly been betrayed.
Where farmer's hands once nurtured seed, death lies in wait.
Weapons of war in heartless hands, planted by men that hate.
Who will tend this crop, when the soldiers finally go
And who will reap the evil, that other men carelessly sow?

Damian Harvey

Friendly Fire

Lies stood and shouted out their hate,
Truth hid behind a wall.
Hate trampled over everyone,
Love wasn't there at all.

I tried to kill my enemy,
I aimed right at his head.
But when I went to bury Lies,
Poor Truth was there instead.

Cindy Jefferies

Weapon Man

On the sighing train
I met a Weapon Man.
How he was designing,
And now he was refining
A rocket, sock-it-to-'em
For his Fellow Man.

Weapon Man, Weapon Man, with arms in his hand,
Weapon Man, Weapon Man, weeping on the Land.

On the crying train
I saw the Weapon Man.
Soon they would be testing,
And bodies would be resting
In peace as part
of a profitable plan.

Weapon Man, Weapon Man, blowing off the hand,
Weapon Man, Weapon Man, crippling the Land.

On the buying train
There sat a Weapon Man.
He was so excited,
His boss would be delighted.
Wow, what a toy!
Biff! Boom! Bang!

Weapon Man, Weapon Man, shuffling his hand,
Weapon Man, Weapon Man, beating the Land.

On the dying train
I heard the Weapon Man.
How his breath was rasping,
Now his heart was gasping
For life. A stroke of bad luck,
As his soul just ran.

Weapon Man, Weapon Man, dealt a dead hand,
Weapon Man, Weapon Man, buried by the Land.

Andrew Fusek Peters

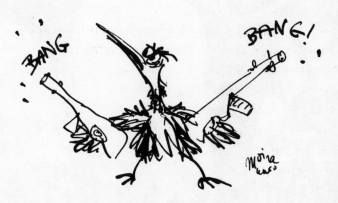

Evolution

I met my foe the other day;
we fought with fist and knee.
We grappled, shouldered,
kicked and roared
till finally, our limbs subdued,
each slunk away.

I met my foe the other day;
he came with fist
and I with sword.
I answered flesh
with sharpened steel,
he sank without a word.

I met my foe the other day;
I brought my dainty gun.
He bared his sword to greet me;
one finger crooked,
my foe was gone.

I saw my foe the other day –
no more than just a blur
across a smoky battlefield.
I saw him fall...
                    or was it her?

I didn't even see my foe –
no faces, no distress.
I pressed the button quickly
and found a wilderness.

Judith Nicholls

Unreasonable People - Myths About Pacifism

Pacifism is simplistic.
Tell me what's simpler – to join an army and learn to do exactly what you're told, without thinking for yourself about issues like wars, terrorism and ethnic struggles, or to have to work it out for yourself, form your own opinions, and then stick to them with everyone else telling you you're wrong.

Pacifism is naïve.
Think peaceful protest never changed anything? Read about Gandhi, and how his methods hastened an end to Imperial Rule in India. Or South Africa, where years of sanctions finally brought an end to apartheid. Or Vietnam, where the vast number of packets of rice sent to the White House bearing the label "drop this on Vietnam, not bombs" so alarmed the administration that they hid the story from the world.

Pacifists are cowards.
Tell that to men like Alfred Evans, who faced a firing squad in World War I for being a conscientious objector. "Men are dying in agony in the trenches for the things they believe in," he said, "and I wouldn't be any the less than them."

Pacifists are unreasonable people.
Well, maybe that one's true. If there's ever any change in the world, it comes from people daring to speak the unorthodox. If they didn't, things would stay the same. "All progress depends on unreasonable people," said George Bernard Shaw.

Pacifism could never happen across the world.
Maybe it could, maybe not, but listen to the logic of the First World War pacifist slogan – Wars will stop when men refuse to fight. Progress depends on individual people sticking to their beliefs: in the words of Gandhi – "We must become the change we want to see."

Marcus Sedgwick

Captive audience

Hope

I found Hope in a newspaper
a week before the war.
Her eyes claimed attention.
I couldn't look away.
So I cut her out and kept her
pinned her on my wall.
I called her Hope
for the light in her infant eyes.

Today I stare at the front page
of the newspaper mom forgot to hide:
at a broken doll
in a blood-soaked shroud
a green soother at its tiny blue mouth
just like the one I used to have.

Later, I make crispy cakes
chocolate clusters
for the school Bring and Buy.
We'll send the money to UNICEF
to buy medicines and food,
bandages and clothes.
It's all we can do
for the children
liberated by terror
in our name.

Counting out pillars of pennies
I rebuild
in my mind's eye:
a market street
cratered
a home
bombed;
the remains
of another child's life.

I watch the news
every night
hoping to find Hope.

Julie Bertagna

Use-Up Missiles

You'd think that there were Use-Up Dates
That governments enforce
On certain kinds of missiles,
And it could be true, of course...

For if you buy big missile stocks
Not paid for by yourself,
And there's no need to use them
So they're lying on a shelf,
Then all the tax-payers' money
That you laid out at the start
To fund their manufacture
And to make the missiles smart,
Might seem a bit suspicious
And quite hard to answer for
Unless you think of something...
And you do! You make a war...
To use the missiles, let them fall
Use the missiles, use them all
That way you'll hardly need defend
Your million billion missile spend...
And then, because the shelves are bare,
You're justified in buying more
And quick! Invent a brand new war
– Give any place and reason for –

To use the missiles, let them fall
Use the missiles, use them all
That way you'll hardly need defend
Another million billion spend.

Just do take care we don't find out
That peace is not what you're about
That secretly you're on the take
From those who all these missiles make
And war is just a Use-Up racket
*That nicely adds to **your** pay-packet?*

Hiawyn Oram

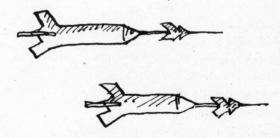

Gas Mask

Playing amongst
the jagged
aftermath
of Granny's garden.
Sharp bits of yesterday
making dangerous toys.
We find, half earth-hidden,
a gas mask,
the shattered, staring eyes
not even winking
in the sun.
This grotesque soft skull
draws us to it.
Such an evil thing
with which to play
and make games of war
and bombs
and silent, coughing clouds.
Putting this fetid thing
to our faces
and pretending
all the terrors of war.

But our game
catches us up
and we wake in screaming sweats,
with the fingers of the mask
still damply clinging to our face.
Such a subtle
creeping
revenge.

Graham Marks

Wars Are Real

Wars are real, you know.
You do know that wars are real?
They're not TV programs
rolling across our screens,
or computer games
you play with friends.
The blood is real.
It's not red ink or raspberry jam.
The bombs are real.
They crush, maim, kill.
Men and women die.
Soldiers die – they're men and women, too,
young mostly.
And children die.
Yes, children die.
And as they die they know not why they die.
And nor do we.
Wars solve little,
but leave behind
a trail of misery and grief.
There must be another way
to resolve differences.
Surely it's better to talk,
and to listen,
to try to close gaps,
to reach across the barricades
and save life,
for life is precious,
for each and every one of us,
no matter which side you're on.

Joan Lingard

My Windowsill

Before I go to sleep I sit on the windowsill;
I like the friendly dark when the world is quiet and still.
I pull the curtains round me and look out at the sky;
I watch the stars come out and the moon go sailing by.

This is my special time, just before I go to bed,
A dreaming time, a time to make up stories in my head.
This is my special place, my window to the sky,
In the peaceful, friendly dark while the moon sails by.

Other children's windowsills have guns and bombs outside;
The children cannot dream and play; instead they cry and hide;
And the night-time is not peaceful and smoke blots out the sky,
In the noisy fearsome dark when the tanks go rolling by.

Tonight I'll make these wishes when I look out at the moon:
That all the guns and all the bombs will stop forever soon;
That all the other children, wherever they may be,
Can sit and dream and watch the sky in safety, just like me.

Sandra Horn

Mr. Shaabi

The polished willow branch in Mr. Shaabi's hand tapped out the rhythm while we chanted the words: Now – is – the – winter – of – our – dis – con – tent.

"No, no," he shouted in irritation. He buttoned and unbuttoned his jacket. "You say these words as if they have no meaning. This is Shakespeare, the greatest poet and playwright the world has known."

A hot wind, carrying the smell of gasoline and burnt rubber blew through the broken glass of the classroom window. My notebook pages fluttered. I laid a ruler across the two sheets of my English lesson to hold them down.

"Who was the greatest playwright, Mahdi?"

"Shay Kesa-peer," I answered.

"One word, Mahdi, one word. This great Englishman's name is one word – Shakespeare. We will recite this famous speech again."

For thirty years Mr. Shaabi had been teaching English in the Saladdin Comprehensive School. My brother and my cousins had been his students. In all those years he never failed to appear, at eight o'clock in the morning, in his jacket and tie. "This is the way a teacher at Oxford greets his students," he would say. "Proper dress shows respect."

Only on the Jewish holy Day of Atonement did he stay home. After the last war his wife took their two daughters and emigrated to Canada, wanting only peace and quiet. But Mr. Shaabi remained. He said nothing. Only Mr. Nurredin, the Principal, received an explanation, "My family and ancestors have lived near the Euphrates for centuries, as far back as 597 B.C. I will not dishonor my history by leaving this city or abandoning my students. Even if I have to live alone."

"Again," Mr. Shaabi said.

Once more eleven of us chanted to the rhythm of the willow branch going up and down: "Now – is – the – winter – of – our – dis – con – tent. Made – glor – i – ous – sum – mer – by..."

The words on my notebook page were black dots, meaningless. All I could think about was tonight. Tonight the bombs would fall again. The television and the radio said we were victorious but the foreign news announced that in twenty-four hours the foreign soldiers, the conquerors, would enter the city. If they came I would shout, "There is nothing for you on my street. Look, everything has tilted or fallen or crumbled or broken or shattered or burned or cracked or twisted or exploded."

I would say to the soldiers, in the English Mr. Shaabi had taught me, "Please leave us alone. My father is an accountant, my mother does sewing at home, my brother is a university student, and I am at the Comprehensive School and my sister is a little girl of five. Only us, we are the only ones left. See, the building is empty. The other six families in our apartment house packed up what they could carry and left for villages outside the city."

But meanwhile here I was, many streets away, sitting in a classroom, listening to Mr. Shaabi drone on in his perfect English accent as if nothing was happening. By tomorrow I could be dead. And my parents, and my brother and my little sister, it was inevitable. Maybe it was even the will of Allah.

To – fright – the – souls – of – fear - ful – ad – ver – saries. Wasn't Mr. Shaabi afraid? Did he think reciting *Richard III* would save us? The air raid siren began to wail.

I looked up from the page, we all looked up. The willow branch in Mr. Shaabi's hand trembled. "None of you have time to get home safely. Take your things and follow me. Quickly."

I grabbed my schoolbag, my notebook, the ruler clattered to the floor. Out of habit we formed our single class line. We ran down the stone flight of stairs, following Mr. Shaabi. I heard screams and shouts from the other classrooms. Mr. Shaabi never turned around. We followed him out the back door and down the narrow street behind our school. I saw his tie fly out to the side like a black flag and his jacket flap against his legs. Where was he taking us? Where were we running to? The high pitch of the air raid siren continued.

I bumped against the other boys as I ran. I heard my breathing. My mouth was dry. I thought I would choke. Could the bombs fall here? Could a pilot in the sky see me? I saw the sign on the corner – Rashid Street. We were in the Old Town. Mr. Shaabi stopped and turned around. "Are you all here?"

"Yes," we answered.

He pushed open a thick wooden door. "Hurry, everyone inside."

When he saw we had all entered, he led us down winding steps to a square whitewashed room. In the dim light I saw rows of benches, a pulpit, and two carved doors. The air raid siren was drowned out by the explosions of bombs, again and again and again. We had reached this place just in time.

I stood behind him. He did not turn to look at me.

He moved forward a few steps to the two carved doors. "Now is the –"

"Oh no," I thought, "he will begin to drone his Shakespeare again."

"– time for me to stand before your Holy Ark, Lord, the place of the Torah scrolls." His English words were slow, and spaced as if he held the willow branch in his hand, "– to beg you, God, to protect these children of Ishmael, and me, a son of Abraham, all of us inhabitants of this ancient land. Amen."

He bowed and stepped away. He turned around and saw me, "Yes, Mahdi?"

What could I say? Should I recite a Shakespeare line that he had taught us?

"Mahdi?"

"I want to say thank you, Mr. Shaabi."

Pnina Kass

Two Deaths

Death comes
to a crowded market place
in a distant corner of
the world,
taking the form of
a slim, sleek-finned, steel-skinned parcel
that
quickly unwraps itself.

Death comes,
a violent surprise,
to un-named, anonymized faces,
bodies,
and is called:
an unfortunate mistake,
regrettable,
collateral damage,
civilian casualties,
probably one of theirs anyway.

Death comes
to a crowded upstairs room
in a near corner of
the world,
taking the form of
a fiery indoor entertainment spectacular
combined with
inadequate safety procedures
and
locked doors.

Death comes,
a violent surprise,
to named, identified faces,
bodies,
and is called:
a tragedy.

Graham Gardner

69

Bang On!

Sunday paper.
Full color picture.
Five columns wide.
The caption reads, "The body of an Iraqi soldier lies
wrapped in a blanket
near a trench on the Faw peninsula following an assault
by British commandos."
End of quote.
The photographer's name is there too.
Right alongside.
What focus!
So sharp you can almost read the label on the blanket.
Bang On! (Well, you can't miss it.)

There are the hands protruding from under the blanket.
So sharp you can see the soldier chewed his fingernails.
Thumbs and forefingers come together in the shape
of a heart.
Right in the foreground.
In your face.
Sharp detail all the way back to the rocks on the horizon.
Sharply printed too.
Four color registration on high speed presses.
Bang On!
All the news as it breaks.
It's easier to look at too.
In a Sunday paper in Australia.
To know it's Over There,

And somebody *else's* son.

Bob Graham

Watching

What happens becomes history,
the events that blast out of TV screens –
war as it happens, like a video game
or an interactive CD Rom.

But this is real,
as real as hanging
my washing on the line,
as real as cooking the supper,
or hoovering the carpet.

Death comes in through the box in the corner,
is it fact or fiction?
Men in camouflage dig through sand,
other men report the effect of exploded bombs.
Everything is mad, all out of kilter.

A woman with a baby
is helped out of the rubble of her home.
We watch her distress,
the chaos of her life,
as she hugs the baby close.

In the TV studio men in suits
talk about strategies.
It's unreal;
you want to tell them to get a life
but this is where they're at.

And while they add commentary
to heat-haze pictures,
a nomad herds goats
among static helicopters
and ocher-colored Land Rovers.

Sue Moules

In Her Hand

The water foamed cold around her ankles. Looking down, she saw the last rays of the setting sun glint off something rosy, jutting from the wet sand. Isabelle bent to pick it up. Another wave rushed in, splashing her legs and soaking her rolled-up jeans. It almost forced the long, reddish shell from her fingers.

"Got it," she said.

"Isabelle. Tide's coming in," called her father from up by the sea wall. She'd been warned that the tide swept unsuspecting tourists off to England.

Isabelle gripped the shell in one hand and ran ahead of the next wave. Omaha Beach was the widest, flattest beach she'd ever seen. Funny name, too, for a French place. Masses of soldiers had died right here back in World War II, including her Great Uncle Thomas, who was buried in the cemetery on the cliff above them.

The war had taken place so long ago. It never seemed real until she saw the white cross with her family's name on it. One of thousands fanning out in geometrically perfect lines.

She stood by her dad in the softer sand up beyond the tide line. The air was growing chilly. The tour director had a small bonfire going nearby and several other families had gathered around it.

Isabelle gazed at the sky over the Channel, deep red and purple and gold. The waves washing up over the wide beach came fast, skirting sideways before rushing back out to the ocean. In the fading light, she thought of all those guys falling dead, here, where she stood. Did the incoming tide sweep them out to sea?

"Look what I found, Dad." She held out the shell. It was no longer red. More a soft gray, smooth but pockmarked, over an inch long, wider at one end.

"Hmmm. Let me see that." He studied it, rolling it over in his hand. "I think this is a human bone," he said gently, his bushy eyebrows high over his eyes.

A human bone!

He handed it to her. "Proximal phalanx." He pointed to the base of his left index finger. A doctor for a father had its advantages. And disadvantages.

"How did it get here?" she whispered.

"Probably from the war. D–Day. They say the beach still gives back the remains of soldiers every year."

"This is a remain?"

"Yes." He smiled at her.

"W-what do we do with it?" She ran her finger over the sanded smoothness of the bone, sharply aware of her own soft flesh. Isabelle squeezed her eyes shut.

She imagined a young man with freckles like hers, light brown hair under his helmet, wet and salty in heavy clothes and a back-pack, clutching a gun. Like her best friend Anna's older brother. Not some old man.

"How about we take it to the caretaker at the cemetery? He can see to it that it's properly honored and buried."

74

Bury a finger bone. Isabelle nodded, feeling strangely heavy. As if her own clothes were waterlogged. She closed her eyes again, her hand around the remains.

She could hear a deafening noise, the Germans firing down on them from the concrete "nests" they'd visited on the cliffs above. So many soldiers. So many bullets. Friends stumbling. Dropping at your side. Gaping wounds and shredded bits of uniforms flapping in the wind. Legs, arms, heads – exploding in sprays of red and chunks of flesh. Fear. Bottomless. Blackness.

"Are you OK, Isabelle?" Her father pulled her close.

She nodded again, took a deep breath, and looked over at the bonfire. The shadows of the people round it danced on the sand. She watched a spark swirl up into the night. A bird or bat's cry made her father glance up, too.

They both looked toward the cemetery on the cliffs behind them in the darkness. Her family was proud of Uncle Thomas. He helped stop the Nazis. But what would he have become if he had lived? Why Uncle Thomas?

Why any of the millions who died?

Isabelle looked at the bone again, gray and lifeless now. She curled her hand gently around it. And for a moment she felt the enormous size of the effort, and the enemy, and the loss and pain.

She was so tiny. And so was what was – In her hand.

Ann Kordahl

Far Be It

Far, far, far
be it from me
this war;

far be it from me
to sieve the news
for poetry.

But the boy who bled
from his stumps of arms
and wasn't dead

held the shape of the crucifix
they put round my neck
when I was a kid.

On my knees I genuflect,
shaking with rage and shame,
at the TV set.

Carol Ann Duffy

The Singer And The Song

Once in the service of the High King of Elb, there was a musician named Lark. He could play the plekta till its three strings rang like thirty. He could blow the tenor netto till it wailed like a woman in labor. And when he sang, his voice was so pure, it was said that he spoke a hundred truths in a single breath.

Everyone loved Lark, but none more than the young prince of Elb. Whenever he heard Lark sing, the prince would put his small hand in the musician's, look up at him, and say, "Oh, Lark, you are the fairest and truest of all the men in my father's kingdom."

On hearing that, Lark would squat down on his heels so that he could look the boy right in the eye. "Do not confuse the singer with the song, my prince," he would say.

The prince did not believe him, of course. Princes believe what they will. But many years later, on the day the poor folk of the land rose up against the High King, Lark made a song for their victory. In it he rhymed "tyrant" in a dozen different ways, which one could do in the old tongue.

"I thought you were true," whispered the prince to Lark, when they took the entire royal family out of the dungeon to be hanged. "I thought you were the fairest in the kingdom," the prince said as the rope was put around his neck.

But Lark did not answer. He only smiled at the prince. For he had never confused the king with the crown, the rope with justice, or the singer with the song.

Jane Yolen

To The Men Who Plan War

You think there's nothing in the desert?
Nothing there but rats?

Listen to me.
There's a girl with huge hurt eyes there in the desert.
There's a stink with no water pipes to carry it away.
There's fear in the pit of the belly
and only a billowing fire of oil to see by
there in the desert.

But listen to me now.
This is what could be there in the desert.

Trees with finger leaves could burst into lush brown fruit there.
A sky flecked with clouds of pale pink could stop your breath there
just after dawn. That child now running across the grass
could whirl, and throw the ball, and be a proper child there,
not touched by you. A woman could lie soft with her child there,
men play strange games with counters,
smoke rise from fires as food is cooked there.
Yes, a foot could kick a ball there, just like
your grandson kicks his football at home.

Never say there is nothing there.
Listen to me.
Think.

Alison Leonard

Nilly 7

Every day, the war strikes at our newspapers,
Drones like machine gunfire, over radios,
Explodes onto the covers of magazines,
Blasts and bombards its way onto our TVs.

It is horrifying, terrifying, and
We watch with the pain of utter helplessness.

My granddaughter is 6, but writes, "Nilly 7."

We show her Iraq on her plastic globe, and say,
"That's where they're fighting. It's a long way away."
She nods. Then, one night, sees for herself the news
And seeking reassurance, asks,
"That's only a show. Isn't it?
There's not really a war going on?"

Vashti Farrer

War And *The Simpsons*

The really good thing about war is that they generally put
it on at 6 o'clock
Same time as *The Simpsons*.

And nowadays, of course, war is quite safe.
It stays in the TV and makes no mess.
Even if it gets too noisy you can just turn down the sound.

(If you can find the remote.)

Also it is very clean.
No dust, nor smoke, nor blood leaks through the screen.
And when it gets boring you can switch over and watch
The Simpsons.

(If you can find the remote.)

(*The Simpsons* is ALWAYS excellent. NEVER boring.)

The only trouble is, it still goes on.
(The war, not *The Simpsons*. *The Simpsons* lasts for
twenty minutes – unless it is a special.)
The war still goes on. The noise and the smoke and
the leaking blood. The dirt and the boredom and the fear.
You cannot switch it off with the remote.

(Even if you can find the remote.)

You have to switch it off another way
You have to say, No
No
No war
You have to say No To War.

Then you can watch *The Simpsons*
In peace.

Hilary McKay

strange meetings

Heads On The Pillow

Saida lays her head on the pillow. Her hair is black and tousled. Her eyes are deep brown. In her dream the pillow is thousands of kilometers thick. It runs through the earth, through clouds and blue skies. It is so soft she could sleep forever. But sleep doesn't even last for an hour before the air raid siren starts to wail. Then the bombs start to thump the ground like the fists of angry gods. The blasts shake the ground so hard dust falls on her face. Within minutes her parents are in the room scooping her out of her bed. She knuckles the sleep from her eyes. It scares her to hear the fear in her parents' voices. Then Saida hears a huge crash and watches the fireflash of an explosion light her father's face. As they disappear into the cellar next door she tastes the oil smoke from fires on the edge of the city. She smells it burning. It stinks.

Sadie also lays her head on the pillow. Her hair isn't black and tousled. It is blonde and straight. Her eyes are blue like the sky. She wakes up in the middle of the night, as if shaken by shock waves. They seem to come from her pillow, but also from the earth and from the sky. Did I dream it, she wonders. Then she remembers her father flying bombing raids half a world away. Will he come home safe? Could his plane fall from the sky tonight, or will it just be his bombs that fall? She imagines the light of the bombs on her father's face. She imagines the burning. What is it like to drop the bombs? What is it like to be in the city below?

There is no breakfast for Saida the next morning. She is woken by the cries of women dressed in black. They echo round the room like the shrieks of a trapped bird. She calls for her mother, her father too. Wondering where they've gone, she goes to the door and steps into a nightmare. Outside, the world has caught fire. Familiar buildings are burning, their windows knocked out so they look like empty eye sockets, their walls scorched and gutted. Saida walks out under a blood-red sky and gags on the oil fires. Her eyes sting and her throat burns. They stink. She kicks a sandal and sees a bloodstain on the ground where it lay. It shines fresh as if life is still bubbling in it. She looks a little further ahead and terror rises in her throat. Some things you should not see.

Sadie is drawn down to breakfast by her mother's voice. Mom is squealing with delight, "It's your daddy," she says. "Look, it's your daddy." Sadie glimpses him on the aircraft carrier, pulling off his helmet. Before Sadie can see his eyes or that warm smile of his a reporter is looking into the camera, talking about sorties and targets. Sadie isn't interested. She just wants to see her father again. But the report has moved on. Sadie looks outside at the familiar buildings, gardeners burning weeds and stuff. She smells the burning.

It reminds her of something, but what?

Saida finds her father. He is bending over something, squeezing tears from his eyes. Sensing her standing behind him, he hugs her to him. He folds her face deep in his clothes, pressing her so tight she can hardly breathe. It is as though he can't let her out from there, as if he dare not let her eyes see what the world has become. "Where's Mother," she asks. "Did you find her?" Her father doesn't reply but the shaking of his sobs tells her all she needs to know. Suddenly there is darkness in the light of day. Around the city the oil fires still burn, but there are new fires now. They are closer. They lick Saida's heart.

Sadie comes home from school. The TV news is on. She sees a woman wrapped in a blanket, being carried by a group of men. The blanket is slick with red blood. A man and a tousle-haired child follow behind the

woman's body. For a moment the girl's brown eyes seem to look right into Sadie's blue ones, as if they have thought the same thoughts, as if their heads have shared the same pillow, as if they have dreamed the same dream, screamed at the same nightmare.

That night Saida can't sleep. She sobs into a pillow which seems to be thousands of kilometers thick. The earth shakes with her sobs. The sky shines with her tears. Sadie hears the sobs, feels the tears on her face. She sits up a while, wondering if her father is flying tonight and when she lays her head down she can smell the oil burning.

It stinks.

Alan Gibbons

To Have And Have Not

The March sun shines in Georgia, Tennessee, and
    California.
Nieces, nephews, and godchildren ring from the US.
They catalogue their latest acquisitions: new car here,
    designer clothes there, the latest computer gear and
    games, car CD player, costly cell phones.

These children on the phone, these children that I love,
    never mention the war,
The war their unlawfully elected president and his
    henchmen wage against another unlawfully elected
    president and his henchmen.

These US teenagers plan no marches to protest against
    the murders carried out in their names.
They express no anxiety for those outside, or inside, their
    immediate circle.
They focus their attention on choosing the right
    university.
The issue of the moment is color. Should the new car be
    blue or silver?

They have so much, these children of the US.
They have so much, and yet they feel so little.

This March, bombs rain down on Baghdad, Basra,
    and Tikrit.
Iraqi infants, toddlers, and teenagers cry and die on
    the TV news.

The reporters catalog the suffering of these children: they
	have lost a leg here, an eye there, both arms;
	one dead grandparent here, two dead parents there;
	they have no food, no water, no brothers or sisters left
	alive, no hope that things will soon be better.

These children on the news, these children who break my
	heart, never mention freedom.
They do not speak of oil or weapons of mass destruction
	or presidential elections, lawful or unlawful.

Their anxiety centers on the bombs that fall nightly,
	bombs that somehow don't count as weapons of
	mass destruction.
Red, not silver or blue, is the color of the moment: the
	blood that runs down the walls, as well as the blood
	unavailable for surgery to save a dying baby sister the
	US marines shot by mistake.
There is no one giving blood at the hospital. There is
	no hospital.

They have so little, these children of Iraq.
They have so little, and yet they feel so much.

Perhaps if we bought our children a little less and taught
	them to feel a little more,
The bombs might not keep falling on the just and the
	unjust alike.

Robbie Butler

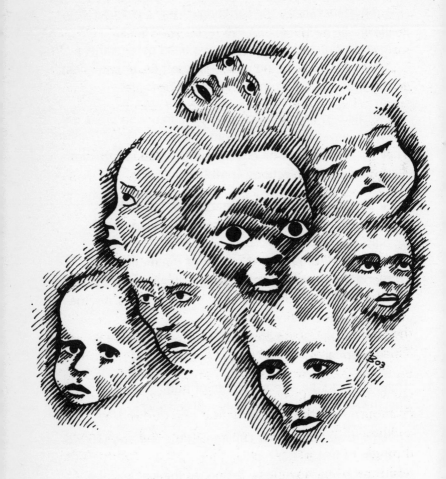

A Night In The Lost Marshes Of Iraq

In the old days, the great marshes of Iraq stretched for hundreds of miles, a mysterious wet landscape alive with life, where people known as Marsh Arabs lived on floating islands made of reeds, and fished from their canoes.

My husband, David, and I went to visit a friend once, on his floating reed island. He was a man called Abbas, and he and his family welcomed us with the great warmth of Arab hospitality.

I wrote a diary of our visit. Here it is.

We made the journey to Abbas' island after dark, when the full moon had risen over the Marshes. On either side of the waterway, the reeds made criss-crossed mazes of shadows. We could see no further than a meter or so, but we could hear the rustling of life, the splash of a fish, the flutter of a bird, or the passage of a rat or snake. Lights from the many small islands glowed softly across the water.

We reached Abbas' island, and were taken at once up the stairs to the roof of his family's new brick house. Thin mattresses and mats were laid out, with cushions on them. There was an oil lamp in the middle of the circle. We were given the place of honor against the cushions, and the whole family sat around us, the children jostling for a good place and squirming through the adults, wriggling into comfortable positions, using anyone's lap to climb into or anyone's shoulder to lean against.

Abbas' little daughter began to show off more than he liked. He said to her, very gently, "Be gentle with

93

our guests. They are foreigners and they don't know us. Be kind and quiet. Don't get over-excited."

In the family circle was Abbas' old mother, his wife, his son and beautiful daughter-in-law, and several children and grandchildren.

Above us, the great black dome of the sky was lit with a vast treasury of stars, the moon hanging on the horizon like a vast yellow melon.

"Is it true that men have walked on the moon?" Abbas asked David.

"Yes," we said, and we all fell silent, almost unable to believe it.

A child asked Abbas if the moon was lit by electricity, and Abbas showed him how the moon turned round the earth and the earth turned round the sun, using the oil lamp to represent the sun and the water jug to represent the earth. Then we screwed up our eyes, and tried to make out the mountains on the moon.

We located Mars, up there in the sky, and David explained what the scientists had discovered.

"Is there any air up there? Any wind?" Someone asked.

I thought to myself, "People have stared up at this night sky for thousands of years, and wondered."

This place, Iraq, was where civilization first began. Farming was invented here. Cows and sheep and goats were all domesticated here. It was here that writing was invented, and the first cities were built. We owe all that we are to Ancient Iraq.

Everyone was beginning to yawn, and the children's heads were nodding.

"Do you want to sleep now, or later?" Abbas asked.

We said we were ready now, and we left the roof while the women made up the beds. When we climbed back up the narrow stair, two mattresses had been laid out side by side with sheets over them, and a pillow for each of us. A double quilt lay folded ready, in case it was cold in the night. Abbas' wife and beautiful daughter-in-law were waiting for me. They made me lie down, then began to massage my legs, pressing the calves and thighs with soothing, rhythmic movements. It felt wonderful.

When they'd finished, they rigged a mosquito net over us, so that we were in a little white world of our own, with the stars above, and the moonlight shining softly through. Giggles and scuffles went on outside, as the family set out their own mats and lay down for the night. An arm was suddenly thrust through into our little cocoon, and a hand dropped a nightdress for me. It was huge, made of heavy cotton, and smelled of camphor and fresh air. I undressed and climbed into it, then, in the wonderfully cool night air, we lay and watched the stars circling slowly overhead, until we fell asleep.

The government of Saddam Hussein drained most of the great marshlands years ago. There is only dry, arid land now where the reeds used to blow in the wind. The Marsh Arabs were made homeless. They have suffered greatly in the last twenty years. Nothing can bring their marsh homeland back. War can only make their suffering worse.

Elizabeth Laird

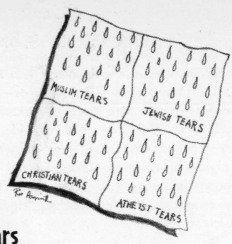

River Of Tears

A river of tears flows by my door
Tears of the wealthy, tears of the poor.
Tears of the many, tears of the few
Tears of the Muslim, the Christian, the Jew.
Tears of the Atheist, Hindu and Sikh
Tears of the powerful, tears of the weak.
Tears of the powerless, tears of the strong
Tears of all nations
– this river is long.

I cry for the children who I might have known
if they had all lived, if they had all grown.
I cry for their laughter unheard evermore
And I add my tears to the river of war.

Ros Asquith

Yield! Narrow Passage Ahead

I live in a suburb of Jerusalem. My cousin in America says it sort of looks like his neighborhood in Baltimore. But there are some big differences.

The other day I was in a rush to get home. But when I reached my bus stop, I saw that it was gone. All that was left was a burnt pole in the ground, nothing any bus driver would recognize as a sign to stop. I must have looked pretty dumb standing at a charred pole by the side of the road. I stepped aside, cringing as the glass crunched beneath the soles of my running shoes.

The splintering glass brought back the images I'd seen on the TV the day before. My mom had been glued to the set.

"What's going on, Mom?"

"Another Arab suicide bomber," she said. "He blew himself up at a crowded bus stop." She began to cry and I could see all the emotions that flashed across her face, sadness mostly, but also anger and frustration.

I turned back to watch the TV as my mother turned away. The television crew had arrived within minutes. Charred body parts were strewn on the ground, broken shop windows with signs saying "Tourists Welcome," and a bicycle that was so twisted up I didn't think it could ever get straight again.

"Why?" I asked her.

"Because Danny, some people simply don't want peace. They think only acts of violence show power."

She shuddered, "It takes more courage to make peace than to strike out in anger."

I went outside to get some air, and to think. I thought about all the Jews who have lived in Israel for generations, and about others who have immigrated here from every continent on the globe. Though most of the time Jews and Arabs have fought, there were times when we lived peacefully together. I know that there are Palestinian Arabs who resent that Jews are living on land that they claim belongs to them. And I know that Palestinian suicide bombers are terrorists who think that they can get what they want by bombing buses, crowded cafés and shopping malls. But don't they know that violence doesn't make people want to speak peace, that it just encourages hate?

Anyway, there I was still standing by the remnants of my bus stop and I needed to get home.

It wasn't far, but as I turned the block a feeling of panic grabbed me. There, walking toward me on the empty street, was a Palestinian.

I'd seen him a few times before. He's about my age and works afternoons at our neighborhood grocery store. But times have changed and where once we might have said hi, now we know we're enemies.

I cursed myself for taking a short cut through the narrow passageway. The sidewalk is uneven with barely room for one to pass. Two could never fit.

One of us would have to yield.

Usually I'm pretty easy-going, but seeing him

walking down the street toward me, I suddenly got this really strange feeling inside me. Maybe it was anger? Maybe it was hate? But all those scenes of mothers crying over their children came flashing back at me. My fists clenched. I squared my shoulders, flexed my pecs.

And I saw him do the same.

I saw his anger at the injustices he felt we had done to him and his people. And I knew we were heading for a showdown.

We met dead center.

But before either one of us could strike, a thunderous explosion shook the ground.

A bomb blast!

Like puppets, our bodies were hurled up into the air. As I landed, I heard the bone in my ankle snap. My cries for help were swallowed up by the commotion somewhere close by. And then I saw him. The expression on his face twisted in pain.

Another boom. Another crash!

We had to hurry and find cover. I scrambled onto my one good foot. He grabbed my hand. I stretched my arm around his back. Hobbling across the street we reached the park.

"You're bleeding," he said.

My knee was oozing gross black stuff and stung so hard it made my eyes water.

"You don't look so great either," I said. "Are you okay?"

That's when he kind of snickered, which caught me off guard. Here we were, lucky to still have all our limbs attached. I didn't see anything funny about it.

"This is nothing," he said. "When I get home, my mom's going to kill me!"

For a second I didn't get it, and then I did! My mom was probably listening to the news at that very second, wondering why I wasn't home yet. And it was so weird, because at that moment I realized that the same thoughts were going through his head and his mom was probably thinking the same thing as mine.

"Boy, are we in big trouble."

I almost wanted to laugh. In some crazy way, we were both on the same side thinking, what a waste! To get home bloody and bruised after a great game of soccer would be worth all the pain. Instead there was no game, no winners, and no referees to call it quits.

"This stinks," he said.

"It sure does," I said. We both heard the sirens, but it would take them a while to find us. He was looking at his elbow. It stuck out pretty oddly. I could tell he was trying to ignore the pain.

"What's your name, anyway?" I asked.

"Chamid," he said.

"Hi," I said. "I'm Danny."

Anna Levine

The Attic

There were nine of us,
ten, if you count the baby.
We crouched, trembling like trapped deer,
listening to the SS searching pitilessly below.
The infant, infected maybe by our fear, began to cry.
"Shut it up!" I said in an urgent whisper.
But the father who held it could not stifle its cries.
"Do we all have to die because of your child?"
my cousin said.
He dragged the baby from its father's arms.
The father's wild eyes,
already as large as begging bowls because of hunger,
stared, as my cousin wrapped his coat
tightly around the little head.
By the time the soldiers went away,
the child was dead.

Nigel Gray

Digging

We were digging to Australia. The three of us. Then it was always the three of us. A summer evening. The thick, ripe smell of pigs, familiar, unnoticeable, drifting over the stile from the cherry orchard. Soon it would be time to go in and watch *Rawhide*. I was in love with Rowdy. When we played *Rawhide* I was always being rescued by him, or I was him. Helen was too weedy to be one of the men and Martin found it difficult to be more than one. Otherwise they were quite pliable. Usually.

"How much more do we have to dig? Frannie?"

"Mmm?" I was wiping a fragment of blue china on my skirt.

"You said when we got to the same height as our shoulders. Look, Martin'll be there in a minute."

"He's the shortest though."

"So?"

"Do you want to stop, Martin?"

"If you like." He was always too easy-going.

"When my mom shouts, we'll stop."

We carried on digging. The moon loomed up big, pitching above the roofs of the cottages. Bats scooped and flittered over the clumps of stinging nettles between the brick lavatories.

"What'll we do when we get there?" One of Helen's favorite questions.

"Explore," I said. "That's what we are. Explorers.

103

Remember?"

"I know what I'm going to do," Martin smiled a slow half-secret. He wanted me to ask.

"What?"

"Start a new life. That's what people always do. Don't they? Least, that's what Mom says."

Until Helen moved in next door, Martin was my only playmate. Our cottages were a couple of miles from the village. A mile and a half if you walked across the gooseberry field. I was always looking out for babies emerging from under one of the bushes there. Being an only child was sometimes a lonely business. When Martin came it was like suddenly having a brother.

It was Martin who taught me how to play French cricket, who bundled in the back of our old Austin van for trips to the seaside where we'd dig our fingers into the bubbling mud, searching for the elusive cockles. Usually we gave them away to the serious hunters with buckets. Somehow they had first claim. My dad said it was only right.

Soon after we'd moved up to Juniors one of the girls had caused some sort of scandal. It was said she showed her knickers to a couple of the bigger boys. Although I sniggered and tutted with the others I couldn't really understand what the fuss was about. I sensed the only way to find out was to try it.

One Saturday we were playing in our camp, among the shoddy sacks, tucked up against the barn eaves. It was where I'd once scratched my arm on a rusty nail and hadn't died of blood poisoning. We always felt secure there, hidden away on top of the shredded remains of other people's clothes, which would one day manure the hop gardens. I was wearing my pink and blue check knickers. A quick flash of my old catalog frock, Martin staring expectantly and it was over. I just felt hot with the naughtiness of it. That was all. He never told.

We hadn't long had a television. Mostly I survived on a diet of *Rawhide, Champion, the Wonder Horse* and *The Flowerpot Men.* Sometimes though, creeping down with a sudden thirst after bedtime, I'd wangle a look at some of the forbidden stuff, the newsreels which flickered late at night.

It was only twelve years since the end of the war. Now pictures of this recent and terrible history provided a novel, instant drama. One thirsty night I glimpsed some awful figures shadowing the corner of our front room. Very thin people, like skeletons dressed in funny, stripy shirts, staring at me from behind barbed wire. Hardly moving. Horrible and staring. At me. I woke up in the night shouting for my mom and when she came I cried and couldn't tell her why.

Not long after I was being a trapeze artist on my swing. Dad was digging over a bit of garden. Mom was pegging out some washing.

"Good morning," It was Martin's mom. Except it sounded like, "goot morgen" to me. She had a strange accent. I liked its sharp edges. She looked different too. Shining blonde, blue-eyed. My mom called back. She wasn't that friendly with Martin's mom, even though they had to work together in the fields. I began to notice that my mom would say scornfully to my dad, things like, "And she says she never knew about them. She must have known."

"Known about what?" I asked once, skipping by, catching her unawares.

"Them awful camps. Poor souls, even the little kiddies. Terrible." Then her face went tight and she sent me off out to play.

The three of us were swinging on the big, old pine tree opposite my house. We were practicing for our circus game. Looking for some sawdust glamour on the familiar grassy bank. The question nagged at the back of my throat.

"Martin?" He was swinging backwards and forwards over my head. I hesitated, not really sure what I was asking. "Your mom."

"Yes?"

"Did she know about those poor people, then?"

"What people?"

"In them places. Camps."

"I know," said Helen, "they had to wear shirts with stripes, like convicts. My dad said they were all gassed. The Germans gassed them." I was suddenly shocked.

"I don't know what you're on about." He'd started to swing so hard. I thought, "If he lets go, he'll end up across the road in our garden."

"Fran-nie! Din-ner time!"

We all jumped down. Martin's gate had already clicked shut behind him by the time I called out.

"See you. Later?"

He didn't answer, but perhaps he knew then. He knew I wasn't sure if I meant it.

Linda Sargent

In The Schwartzwald

They take her brother to break her pride.
She tears splinters from the barracks bed
to still the hunger that gnaws inside.

Through the iron gate, past the words:
Arbeit Macht Frei, she watches guards
throw loaves of bread to the birds.

Not even famine can make barbed wire
seem a candy house she could devour.
The guard tells her: *Child, climb into the fire.*

Gretel tells the guard: *Show me how.*
But the witches are not fooled so
easily in the camps at Dachau.

Lawrence Schimel

Heartmines

"**M**issed!" I yelled, as Toni's ball went spinning past the goalpost and off up the street. It was the summer holidays, and Marko, Katica, Lucija and I were playing soccer against Toni, Branimir and Andreja. I was in goal, and our team was two-nil up.

The ball came to a stop at the feet of a boy of about our age – ten, maybe eleven – whom I hadn't seen before. When it reached him, he steadied it with his foot, then he gave it a kick. And it sailed straight past me into the goal.

Toni was ecstatic. "Hey, Pero!" he shouted to me. "Call yourself a goalie?"

Then he turned to the stranger. "What's your name?"

"Petar."

"Do you want to play, Petar? There's only three of us, and Pero's team has four."

"Okay," came the reply.

The game went on all afternoon, and Petar was brilliant. He told good jokes too. He seemed really nice.

Then Lucija asked the question that changed everything.

"Where did you live before you came to Osijek, Petar?"

"In Belgrade."

Suddenly it was as if a big, dark cloud had descended over everything. I could feel how we withdrew.

"What's wrong?" asked Petar. "Why are you looking at me as if you've seen a ghost?"

"Not a ghost," said Toni coldly. "A Serb!"

"So?"

"The Serbs attacked the Croatians," said Katica, Toni's sister. "They killed our father. You're a murderer!"

"What are you talking about?" Petar said. "I didn't kill anyone."

"No, but your father did! Go away!"

"But I want to be friends!" Petar was looking for help in my eyes. I looked away.

"Come on, you lot," said Toni to the rest of us. "I know a field in Tenja where we can play. It's much better there."

I hesitated for a moment, feeling torn. I liked Petar, but a Serb is a Serb. And besides, I'd grown up with Toni and our gang. I didn't want to lose them.

One after another, they left. Then I too turned to go.

We left Petar standing by himself.

We walked nearly a kilometer, with Toni leading the way and the little kids trailing behind. Eventually, Toni stopped beside a broad stretch of grass.

"Here we are!" he said.

The field was next to an old school. The windows in the building were black and empty, but the grass was smooth and green, and there was plenty of room to run.

Toni started organizing us, fussing about which of the girls would be on which team, and where the sweaters would go for the goalposts. Then the little kids decided they wanted a rest before we started to play. All in all, it was 20 minutes or so before we were ready to start.

Then Toni kicked the ball into the middle of the grass and headed after it.

Suddenly a voice called out, "Stop! It's dangerous!" Toni turned round to see Petar. He had followed us.

"I thought I told you to go away," said Toni.

But then he fell silent. Behind Petar, somebody else appeared. It was my father.

He grabbed me by the shoulder, and shouted at me, "What's the matter with you? Can't you read? What does that say?"

Beside the field, partly hidden by the bushes, was a grey and red sign.

Minsko polje! (Minefield!)

"Well?" my father demanded.

"Minefield!" I mumbled.

"You know you're not allowed to play here!" Father said, looking at each one of us. "Katica, Toni, go home immediately! Hold the little kids' hands. And stay on the path. Go!"

I wanted to go with them but my father held me back. Then he turned to Petar.

"Thank you," he said. And I think he was crying.

My father and I walked home in silence. We left the ball in the middle of the minefield.

That night, there was a huge row. My mom and dad wanted me to go to Petar's apartment and thank him.

"But he's a Serb!" I cried. "You always told me not to talk to Serbs. Not to play with Serbian children. And now you want me to say thank you to one?"

"He may be a Serb," said my dad. "But he saved your life. You could be dead by now if he hadn't come and told us you were going to play in a minefield."

"He would know all about minefields, wouldn't he." I said angrily. "Because it was his father who put the mines there to kill us."

"Not just his father," said my dad.

"Who else?" I asked with surprise. "Who but the Serbs would do something that stupid? Who else would mine a soccer field so that kids can't play on it?"

There was a pause. Then my father said quietly, "Us."

"You?" I felt as though the breath had been knocked out of me. "Who?"

"Our soldiers laid landmines," said Dad. "And so did I."

I was stunned. "Why? Why would you do something so stupid?"

"Pero!" yelled my mom. "Don't you dare talk to your father like that!"

My dad didn't yell. He just turned and walked out.

Why did my father lay mines in his own town? Mines that would kill and hurt not just the enemy's soldiers, but his own friends, his own children?

My Granny tried to explain. "He did it because he wanted to protect you," she said. "He wanted to protect all of us. He thought it was the right thing to do."

Granny told me that during the war, Tenja saw some of the worst fighting between the Croatian and the Serbian armies. Both sides used landmines to stop the enemy.

"And now?"

"Now that the war is over, we must get help to take the mines out of the ground. Until we do, it's not safe for children to play or people to work the land, or even walk across it."

"But first we must take the mines out of our hearts," Granny said. "We must make friends. That's why your father wants you to thank Petar. Someone has to start."

"Yes, but why me?" I demanded bitterly. "Why not Toni and Katica and the others?"

"Toni and Katica would find it even harder than you do," replied Granny. "Before they came to Osijek, they lived in a place called Vukovar. The Serbs destroyed their home and killed their father. It will be a long time before Toni and Katica can take the mines out of their hearts."

The next day I was standing in front of the door of Petar's apartment, my heart pounding. Behind me, the others were trying to be as small as possible.

Finally I found the courage to knock. The door opened. It was Petar. He was surprised to see us.

"We've come to say thank you," I said in a small voice, "Thank you for saving our lives." One less heartmine.

Petar smiled. "That's okay," he said.

"And we want to say sorry," I said. Another heartmine less.

"I'm sorry," Marko said. And another.

"We're sorry too," said Branimir and Lucija.

"Sorry," said the others.

We turned to go.

"Wait," said Petar. "You might need this!" and he held out a soccer ball. "Yours is still in the minefield. But you can have this one."

"Great!" said Bran. "Thanks."

"Will you come and play with us?" I asked.

"Okay," said Petar. "I'll just get my sweater."

Sabina Horvat

Bryn y Mor / Baghdad

A crowd of people round a tank,
And a boy in a red sweatshirt,
Waiting for food or water
Or something to happen.
Smaller than me, darker than me,
Thousands of miles from the Swansea Valley.
I'd be angry, hungry, terrified there.
But where did he get our sweatshirt,
Our blood-red Bryn y Mor sweatshirt?

Malachy Doyle

Masks

The front doorbell rang just as I was going to get my Halloween costume and make-up on. Mom wouldn't let me go trick or treating, but she was letting me have a Halloween party for a few girls I'd got to know at my new school.

I sighed, not wanting to open the door. It was too early for it to be my friends. I knew who it was before the flap of the letterbox rattled as someone banged it over and over again. Taulant and Emira, the Kosovan kids from next door. If I let them in, they'd see all the party stuff and then Mom would go on at me again about how it wasn't nice not to invite the children next door. She didn't understand they were just little kids. They wouldn't fit in at a Halloween party with us big ones.

Emira called my name through the letterbox. Usually the minute they saw us come home, they'd be around, ringing the bell, banging the letterbox to be let in. Dad had put a little latch low on the outside of the back garden gate so they could let themselves in if they wanted to play with my old toys in the shed, but most times they came into the house.

Usually I didn't mind. Emira was really cute, with her big red cheeks and loads of shiny brown curls. And Taulant wasn't into breaking things like boys his age usually are. But I'd spent ages decorating the sitting room like a spooky cavern and making grungy-looking food for the table. Emira would ruin everything, spreading the floor with the writing and drawing stuff that Mom kept for them in a special cupboard in the sitting room. And she'd want me to read to her again. I didn't have time for that.

While I stood there on the stairs, thinking what to do, I heard Taulant come along and whisper to Emira. Then the bell rang again. I tip-toed upstairs. Mom wouldn't come down because she'd be expecting me to let them in. If I ignored them, they might go away.

They didn't. They rang the door and banged the letterbox some more. Mom shouted for me to let them in. I pretended not to hear. Finally, I heard them leave. I felt a bit bad, but I thought I might go around later and take them some cakes and sweets and their favorite books – *Not Now, Bernard* and *The Hungry Caterpillar*. They wouldn't want me to stay to read those. After Mom and I'd read those books to them for the millionth time, Emira knew them by heart.

The doorbell rang again, just as I was about to paint my face. I peeped out of the window. It was just a trick or treater. I went downstairs and opened the door. A witch about my age stood on the doorstep. "You alone?" I asked, surprised. I gave her some of the sweets and coins from the jars by the door.

She nodded. I was going to ask where she lived, thinking Mom might let me go trick or treating with her next year. Then I thought, "I'll be too old for that stuff next year. Probably be taking Taulant and Emira."

I didn't know if they had Halloween in Kosovo, but by then they'd know all about it from living here.

I was trying to get ready again, when I heard a shrill scream, followed by a lot of shouting. Then there was banging on our front door. The witch who'd been at our door a minute ago stood there again. She looked really scary this time, with her make-up running all over her face from her crying.

Mom came down to see what all the fuss was about. The witch just sobbed and pointed next door, where Taulant's whole family was standing on their doorstep. Taulant's father, Enver was shouting a mixture of English and his own language. The mother, Kadija, was crying really loudly, clutching Taulant and Emira who were screaming and crying too.

Mom asked the witch, "What happened? What's wrong?" The witch said, "I didn't do nothing. That man just came at me for nothing." She started saying her dad would sort him out. Mom looked to where Taulant's father was shaking his fist at the girl, shouting at her. The mother was kneeling by the children. She pulled the father down and they put their arms around each other and the children, all holding one another like they were trying to keep inside a magic circle for protection.

Mom patted the witch's head and wiped her face with a tissue. She picked up the jar of sweets and gave the whole jar to the girl. "Here. It's just a joke. They're playing a joke back on you, see? You misunderstood.

Your dad would only call you a silly. You live nearby? Look. That's a lot of sweets. You go home now."

The girl snatched the jar and ran down the road like there were real witches after her. I followed Mom next door.

"What's the problem here?" Mom said. She pulled me to her. "It was just a little girl, like Zora. See Zora. Not real. Only pretend, see?" She kept saying that over and over, pointing to me, in my costume but without my make-up, so they could see the dressing up and the real part of me, but they all went on crying, even Enver.

Mom started moving them inside as she spoke, trying to explain in simple language what Halloween was about. After a while, Enver wiped his face on his sleeve and sat looking at the floor. "Girl frighten Taulant. Frighten my children," he said.

Mom said, "She didn't mean to, really. All the children dress up. They put things on their faces and pretend to scare people. People give them sweets."

"In my country," he said, "People come with..." He didn't know the words for masks and face paint so he moved his hand up and down in front of his face, like he was rubbing something on it. "They look like that. Like girl just now. Thing on face. They take people outside. They shoot."

Mom said helplessly, "No shooting here. Play only."

Enver started crying again, "Taulant frightened. He with my brother. People, they come. Take my brother

outside. Shoot him. Taulant hide. He see people with..."
He made the movement with his hand over his face
"...again. Kadija. Emira baby. See people shoot mother.
Sister. Other people. Not play. Kill. War."

A car stopped outside. I could hear voices shrieking
as people went up our garden path. Enver looked
terrified. He grabbed Taulant and shoved him upstairs.
Kadija grabbed Emira and followed them. They were all
screaming again.

Mom shook her head at me. We opened the door
and went home. We'd left the door open and a load of
vampires and ghosts and witches stood just inside the
door and spilled over onto our doorstep.

"Get inside, quick!" I pushed everyone inside and
quickly shut the door. I didn't want the family next
door seeing a masked gang on our doorstep. I didn't
want them to think people in masks had come to kill us
like people had killed their relatives during the
Kosovan War.

Shereen Pandit and Zora Laattoe

The Bridge at Mostar

Built in the 16th century, the ancient bridge at Mostar, Bosnia has been the subject of thousands of paintings and photographs. In an ethnically divided town, it reached across the river to connect the Croats on the West Bank with the Muslims on the East. In 1993, after standing for nearly 500 years, it was blown up during the Yugoslav Wars.

There was a bridge here.
For 500 years.
There was a bridge.

Children met on the bridge.
Leaned over the balustrade.
Threw stones into the river.
The stones did not care
from which side of the river they had come.
The river did not care.
And the bridge?
It was made of stone.
Bridges do not care.

Friends met on the bridge.
Lazed against the balustrade.
Sipped coffee, ate cake – messily, noisily.
They talked about oh, how it had rained last night.
They talked about a new scarf.
They looked up at the sun.
They laughed.
And when they parted,
they sometimes forgot which side of the bridge
led home.

Lovers met on the bridge.
Sat on the balustrade.
Fingertips touched.
Cheeks touched.
Winds blew across the river.
The lovers kissed
and did not notice the wind braiding their hair.
The wind did not know which side of the bridge
the lovers were from.
Their lips did not know.
But their minds knew.
Always.
And they thought how difficult it was
to be lovers who met on a bridge.
But also how exciting.
And they were grateful
that there was a bridge.

Birds met on the bridge.
Perched on the balustrade.
Sang.
Pecked crumbs left by the friends.
Swooped through the cool darkness below.
Then out again – joyously – into the light.
To the birds the bridge was a place for crumbs.
Each side was the same except
on one they had built a nest.

It was a fine bridge.
An old bridge.

But then the bombs met on the bridge.
The bombs knew nothing of the bridge.
But the men who dropped them did.
The bombs knew nothing about the sides.
But the men who dropped them did.
The bombs knew nothing of the lovers.
But the men who dropped them did.

And now,
There is no bridge.
It is mixed with the stones dropped by the children
At the bottom of the river.
The river does not care.
It does not care for sides.
It feels the sides as it slides by
Like a blind man feels walls.
But it does not feel for the children.
Or the lovers.
Or the bridge.
It flows over the bridge and says
You are mine now.
I will make smooth all that was broken.
I will make you forget
You were a bridge.

That is what rivers do.

The bridge is gone.
The lovers.
Gone.
The friends.
Gone.

A fine old bridge.
It stood for 500 years.

Now there is the river.
And the sides.
And the men with the bombs.

And the children.
Standing on the sides.
Stones in their hands.
Staring at the place.
Where there was a bridge.

Bruce Balan

That Bit Of Sule

Outside, the moon looked like a giant water-gourd. I had never seen the moon that full. I wondered if it was like this in Enugu and I somehow just never saw it. At the thought of Enugu, a city I had lived in until two days ago, a tear trickled down my face. I hastily wiped it with the back of my left hand. It would never do, a boy my age, to be caught crying. That would be my reputation down the drain, for sure. It was hard enough moving, but being considered a cry-baby in a new place would be the absolute pits. I would never be able to live it down. Even if I lived to be a hundred years, nobody would ever forget that.

But I missed Enugu. I missed my home. "Home," I sighed and moved from the window and the new moon and lay back on the bed. This place would never seem like home. No matter how hard Papa shouted and Mama (who did not shout, but whispered or near-whispered according to her mood) tried to drill it into me.

"Kingsley," my father had hurled at me when I had asked when we could go back to Enugu, "this is where I was born. This is where your roots are. This is your home." It did not feel like my roots were here. This dusty village with children who looked at me like I had dropped from Mars.

"King," my mother had said in an affectionate near-whisper, "try to be happy here, okay? You will have fun here."

Later, when they thought I was not listening, my head bent over my Superman comic, I heard Mother whisper to Father, "Papa, Kingsley, he is still a small boy. He does not understand. He is still only ten, eh? Not twenty."

But Father had just grunted and buried his head in a newspaper.

Father had not always grunted and Mother had not always whispered. They both took to grunting and whispering when the talk of war began. I knew what war meant. I had seen it on TV. Soldiers shooting and getting shot. Father did not like me to watch action movies, but they were on every Sunday around the time he took his nap and Mother was away at a Christian Mothers meeting. So I knew what war was, all right. But there were other words flying around that made no sense to me. Grown-up words which the adults spoke reverentially, even as arguments got heated like ground-nut oil for our Sunday morning breakfast of akara balls: Secession. Imperialist. National pride. Oil boom. Oil doom.

Then came the pictures on TV. Houses burning like cardboard paper. Stern-faced generals sounding like my class master.

Then, the adults started acting weird. My best friend, Sule, who lived with his family in the apartment above ours was not allowed to visit me any more.

Father turned him back one Sunday afternoon and announced solemnly to me that Sule was "the enemy." Sule, with whom I had spent every waking day. We went to the same school, were in the same class and lived in each other's homes. Our parents always teased us, calling us each other's shadows.

"But Papa, we did not quarrel. He is my best friend."

Father shut me up with his eyes and grunted, "He is Hausa. He is Muslim. They are killing our people."

When Mother intervened and whispered that I could not understand, Father said it was time I understood. I was his okpala, an Igbo man's first son. I should not be fraternizing with the enemy. I did not know what fraternizing meant, but I knew better than to ask him to explain.

We went to school with name tags stuck on our shirts. Men were asked to join the army and women were asked to have a huge pestle handy for clubbing any enemy soldier who might come into their homes. Sule no longer came to school and an eerie silence settled like fine dust over their apartment upstairs. When I asked Mother why I no longer saw Sule or his parents, she wiped her eyes with the palm of her hand and said I asked too many questions. That night, I sneaked out and crept up to Sule's apartment. The brown door was bashed in, looking all crumpled and the sitting-room was a mass of broken chairs and china.

That night, my nightmares started. I would see Sule, dangerously close to a cliff, calling out to me to help.

Whenever I stretched out my hand to pull him across to safety, women with pestles jeered and hit me with their weapons and I would wake up, screaming.

It was Mother who whispered to Father that we should move. "Things will only get worse," I heard her say. Father grunted his approval and I was bundled into the battered 504 that my father had owned since I was born and we drove the two hours to Osumenyi.

I wanted things to get back to normal. I wanted Mother to talk with a smile like she used to. I wanted my father to lose the grunt. I missed Enugu. I missed my school. But most of all, I missed Sule. I missed going bird-hunting with him. We had identical catapults with which we terrorized birds in our neighborhood. I rummaged in my bag at the foot of the bed and pulled out a blue catapult. Making sure that no one could see me, I held it against my cheek and let the tears flow unchecked. Hot and salty, they came coursing down, wetting my face like warm raindrops. The catapult was Sule's and he had forgotten it in my bag the last day we had gone bird-hunting. I was grateful for that bit of Sule. For even then I knew that I would never see my best friend again. I did not know what would happen in the future, but I knew that nothing would ever be the same again.

Chika Unigwe

Free World

The world lay
In the vast hands
Of the universe
Struggling and fighting,
Like a cornered butterfly.
The universe peered at it
With great curiosity,
Laid one soft finger
On its contorting back
And said;
You are so free
If only you knew it.

Hiawyn Oram

Miracles

I know many people brushed by the Angel of Death in war. But a little silver dust always clings to those who survive, as if the wing of that angel is bright, rather than dark.

As a child at church my eyes always followed one older man. From the left side he looked normal. But from the right you saw he had only one cheekbone, a great hollow gouged in his cheek. Shrapnel from World War I. My eyes scooped down that awesome dip every Sunday. His survival was a miracle.

Another one lucky to survive was my friend Marina. We played squash together, neither of us very good: more giggle and miss than hard splat. But I usually won because at unexpected moments Marina's knee joints would both give way. She would end up suddenly splayed on all fours on the floor, like a frog. Malnutrition as a baby after World War II. Marina's Russian parents had vanished in the Holocaust, and she ended up in a Displaced Persons' camp, along with thousands of other children. But Marina's uncle searched the camps for two years and found her. He and his childless wife adopted her, even though they were in their fifties, and had to bring down their ages by ten years on the application form. Otherwise they would have been considered too old to adopt. Marina is another miracle.

Same as Jacob, a Jewish friend. I once asked him if he

ever wanted to visit Poland, where his parents had come from.

"No" he said, "It's just a graveyard." Jacob himself grew up in Canada, where his immigrant father ran a bakery shop, up every morning at 3.30 a.m. slapping bread dough into fragrant rolls for Canadian breakfasts. Jacob's parents had met deep in a Polish wood, where they had both fled separately to escape the massacres which had killed their first husband and wife, all their relatives, their entire village. They banded together for four years to survive, living rough on berries and roots, unable even in the harshest winter storms to make a fire which might give them away. Love had grown. Jacob and his sister were living miracles to their parents, the yeast of life growing them tall and strong.

Then there's my German friend, Lisabet. Every day she pulls sweet strands of music like toffee from her violin, and coaxes thumb-fingered children to saw bright notes from their curly-scrolled violins. Lisabet's German father was a prisoner of war in a Russian camp for four years, holding hard to the picture and thought of his fiancée. He returned home to his village the very day his fiancée, believing him dead, married someone else. That Lisabet's music breathes perfume into our air is living proof of the new love her father found later with another woman. Lisabet's own bright daughter sings like an angel. The miracles continue.

And me? Ordinary little me, fair-haired and lucky in a lucky land, born to parents who married during

World War II?

I thought the great waves of war that smashed other lives had passed us by more or less unscathed. That I was the most ordinary of miracles, a child born in the sun-dappled calm that followed the war.

Not so. My mother told me her story only when I was grown, one late golden afternoon as we lay on a rug in the sun, under the scribbly-bark tree that arched over our house, its bark scrawled on by insects in a script I tried oh so hard to read as a child.

"A fortune teller once told me I'd have three children," said my mother.

"Then she was wrong," I said a touch wistfully, thinking of the two of us, me and my older brother. How many times I'd begged my mother to give me a little brother or sister!

"Oh no," my mother said. "The fortune teller was right." I stared at her.

"I was pregnant during the war," she said. "It was the darkest time of my life. We'd been married only four months. Greg found out he'd been posted to Brisbane for a month before being sent to fight in New Guinea. I'd just found out I was pregnant, though we had wanted to start our family later. A telegram had come to say my twin brother was dying of appendicitis, way on the other side of the continent.

"Well, I caught my train to Brisbane and halfway there, a soldier pulled down a suitcase from the luggage rack onto my head. It was an accident. But I lost my baby right there on the train. And when Greg met me, he told me he was sailing off to war in two days' time. So two days later I took the train back to Sydney. I walked slowly up the hill to the house, having lost my baby, not knowing if I'd see my husband again, not knowing whether my only brother was still alive. And on the doorstep was a yellow telegram. They meant one thing: someone had died. It was my favorite cousin. Opening that envelope was the lowest point of my life."

I reached out for my mother's hand. She smiled at me.

"But then it all turned out all right, you see. My brother lived — he was the first Australian they used the new wonder drug, penicillin, on. He survived the war, he married and there you have your two cousins. Your father came back after five years in New Guinea and we have you two children. So it was all right in the end. Like a miracle."

"But you always said you only wanted two children," I said slowly. "If that baby had lived, would you have had me?"

She thought. Then, "Probably not," said my mother, and we both fell silent, there on the rug in the sun. The shadows were longer now. I thought of my phantom sibling, whose death meant my life. A butterfly flitted in the garden. And a little silver dust from the bright war-angel's wing drifted onto me too.

Wendy Blaxland

In the ruins

Wallpaper

War is boring, mostly.
When you've seen one ruined house
you've seen them all,
unless of course
it happens to be yours.
You walk through rubble
and you're feeling pretty good
because it isn't you that's dead.
That bomb
didn't have your name on it.
That's what they said.

I never prayed
in case the Namer in the sky
might notice anyone who made a fuss.
Better to keep the head down,
be anonymous.

It was the wallpaper that got to me,
up there where a bedroom used to be.
Fireplace in the middle, mantelpiece –
and nicely round it, violets
or rosebuds like we had,
with satin stripes between.
You weren't allowed to scribble on
the wallpaper, but now
rain fell all over it
and made the colors run.

Alison Prince

Missing

The shell that hit
the busy street market
blew his father and his brother
to pieces

Each night now
in his dreams, he wanders
that heartlorn place, trying to put them
back together

Head, limbs, organs,
he finds the pieces yet cannot
make them fit. There is always something
missing, it seems

Always something

Alan Durant

I Have A Label

I have one small bag
and one small toy.
We're on the train,
one Mom, one boy.
I think it's going to rain.

We're leaving London, Mom and I.
We're leaving home, Mom says to keep us safe.
But what about my house, my friends, my school?

I have a label on my jacket.
I have a label, like a packet.
Mom says it's in case I get lost.
Perhaps they'll put me in the post.

My house is on a narrow road.
We all live close,
we play in the streets.
I don't like the sirens
They're scary.

We're going to Devon
it's a long way away.
Mom says we'll spend all day
on the train
in the rain.

I've never seen a farm
or cows or sheep.
Mom says we can go home
when the war's over.

I hope it's soon.

Hillary Taylor

The Voyage

For refugees everywhere, particularly those imprisoned in Australian detention centers.

Part One: Jasamin's Story

I'd never seen the ocean before, and when the door of the van was swept aside, it was like a rolling blue desert that seemed to last forever. Strong and powerful. And the smell. Like Ahmed's stall in the market. Dried fish laid out in waves and hanging in bunches from thick, curved hooks. Ahmed would laugh with the fishermen and offer them tea. Mom said they'd been on their boats all night.

I'd dreamt of the ocean, but it had never been as beautiful as this.

I heard someone say we were in Indonesia. It was the fifth country we'd been in since we'd left Dad in Iraq. "We were lucky," he kept saying as we hurried through the airport. "To start over is a gift from God." I felt proud God had chosen us for his gift. Dad smiled. Mom looked away. I was angry with her. She'd taught us always to say thank you for gifts and now she said nothing. Dad held me tight and whispered, "Show your mom how brave you can be."

I looked away from the ocean and saw my mother's eyes. Deep and sad. I tried to show her I was brave. I asked where we were, when we were going to eat, when we'd see Dad again, but she said nothing as we made our way to the boat.

I knew something was wrong when the captain started yelling. He screamed in a language I didn't know. He was angry. Scared. Then the rain began. My mother held me tighter and began to pray. I heard whispers that the boat was too crowded. That we were sailing with pirates. The roof was narrow and broken, letting through barrels of water. An old man covered his wife with his coat. A boy beside me started to cry. I grabbed his hand and smiled. I had to be brave. The water spilled onto the deck. It came from everywhere. Rain and waves. Some bigger than the boat. I tried not to let my mother see me cry as the boat tipped sidewards and we were covered by the rising wall of ocean.

Part Two: The Politician's Stomach

The politician put on a brave face as his stomach felt like it was on fire.

"No one can ever know the real story." He was nervous and tugged at his tie like it was a noose. "The public must be told that the Australian government did all they could to save the people who'd drowned. That the boat was illegally sailing in Australian waters and that we are doing our best to protect the Australian borders from people smugglers."

He reached into his pocket for an indigestion tablet.

"It's all been taken care of." His assistant handed him a glass of water.

The politician took the water without saying thank you. He thought the assistant was too young, too cocky, too smiley.

The assistant smiled even wider. "This may even be one of your finest moments and no one will ever know."

The assistant went to the politician's bar fridge and took out a beer.

"And let me be the first to congratulate you."

He held the beer high and took a giant swig.

The politician eyed him with a steely gaze, wondering how he could get him sacked without too much trouble. "You can go."

The assistant's smile faltered. "Sure."

The politician turned away and walked towards the window. "And you can leave that here."

The aide put the beer on a glass-topped coffee table and closed the door behind him.

The politician looked out his window across the rolling green hills beyond his office. As a young man he had loved politics, but now he'd had enough. He clutched his stomach as a sharp pang tore through it like a burning whip. He found it hard to stand up straight. His eyes filled with water, making the hills look like waves. He gasped for breath, like he was suffocating. Like he was drowning.

Part Three: Abraham

Abraham slid down the stairs and ran into the lounge room while his mother yelled again for him to come to dinner. It was Sunday night. The night his family ate in front of the TV. He had to eat quickly because he still had lots to do before the weekend was over. He'd been painting the model boat his dad had bought him and trying to break his record for bouncing his soccer ball on his knee. He was the reigning champion at school and the play-offs were tomorrow to see if he could retain the title.

He sat in his chair next to his dad, his plate on his lap filled with his favorite dish. Leftover ravioli. The TV was on but he heard none of it as he let the first ravioli sink into his mouth. They tasted even better the day after. He chewed and thought about soccer, when he noticed a reporter interrupting with breaking news, with photos of the ocean and a sinking boat.

Abraham's mother handed him a glass of milk. He took it without saying thank you. They all stared at the TV and said nothing. The people from the boat were in the water, crying and afraid, holding up their arms to be rescued. Abraham saw a little girl. She didn't look afraid as she clung to a plank of wood, the boat half-submerged beside her.

Suddenly Abraham didn't feel hungry. The reporter talked about storms, people smugglers and illegal immigrants. There were no survivors.

Abraham left his fork lying on the remaining ravioli. He excused himself and went to his room, the face of the little girl following his every step.

Refugees are ordinary people, forced to flee their homes to escape war and human rights abuses, such as persecution, torture and even death. Under International Law a person is entitled to apply for refugee asylum in another country when they claim they are fleeing persecution.

No one wants to be a refugee and it is up to everyone to protect their lives and dignity.

Deborah Abela

Displaced Persons

We are the forgotten,
The roofless, homeless, voiceless.
We are the slow trudge,
Lugging our clumsy burdens,
Our bagged-up lives.
Our soundtrack, wailing children,
While bombers scour the sky.
Sand tracks, dust roads, highways
Blister our feet and numb our minds.
One step, another. One step, another,
Till checkpoint or collapsepoint
Demands a shambling halt.
Behind is danger. Ahead –
We dream of water, food, a sleeping-place,
However much or little
Survival means.

Victories are elsewhere –
Flags waved, statues toppled,
And cheering, jeering crowds.
We are not asked to choose.

While we tramp the endless roads
History happens behind us.

Linda Newbery

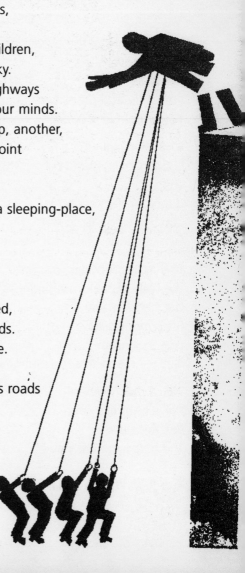

But The Bathroom Has A Lock

But the bathroom has a lock, maybe that will be safe...
Instead, we wait,
In the cellar secure,
In the back of my head there sits fear,
Wearing a robe of darkness

Sound as big as the universe
Tumbles over the sky
Heavy as shame.
I must try and protect my family,
Wrap them in a shield of warmth

A silence explodes,
Sudden as lightning before thunder,
Then
Hard hail hammering on slate
Walls remind me of jelly
Glass departs, doors follow suit

The sound subsides, disperses,
We walk out into nothingness,
We stand in awe and weep
Brick mountains,
Rivers of rubble
And valleys of tossed belongings.

The sound is reborn,
We scatter like mice,
But this time
The bathroom has no lock.

Year 9, Sir William Borlase School, with Andrew Fusek Peters

Out Shopping

I didn't hear the siren!
But the bomb came whistling down.
Mom pushed me into the bushes
And the iced buns rolled away.
She threw herself on top of me
To save me from the blast.

The ground shook like a cakewalk
But Mom lay so still on top;
Till they ran from the shop,
Saw the state of her head –
And brought a huge white table cloth.

At Casualty I was a "cut and graze"
But they took Mom somewhere else,
Where news came round a tight-held door
For only Dad to hear.

I slept at Auntie Ethel's,
Praying in a cold hard bed,
When Dad came in from the landing's glow
To tell me Mom had gone.

To heaven.
On 14th January 1941.

It wasn't shrapnel, a bullet, a shell
That killed her out shopping with me.
It was a tile from the roof of St Saviour's Church
Where we used to pray for peace.

Bernard Ashley

Collateral Damage

When Abu Ziad,
Baghdad accountant,
saw the ankles
of women and children
scored with blood-bracelets
from climbing
over red-hot mattress springs
to escape the inferno
and boiling water
from the tank
sliced by the first bomb
that pierced the roof
of Amiryia shelter,
the bottom had already fallen out
of his profit and loss account.

It was the second bomb
that deprived him
of identifying
Zena (14)
Faud (12)
Lena (7)
Sadaad (6)
and his wife.

Beverley Naidoo

With thanks to journalist Maggie O'Kane reporting on meeting Abu Ziad, an elderly accountant in Baghdad, seven years after his family was killed in the first Gulf War.

Guernica

On April 26th, 1937 an event happened that shocked the world. The tiny town of Guernica in Northern Spain was bombed in broad daylight on market day. For three hours the planes of the German Condor Legion bombed the town and strafed the people as they ran out of the buildings and tried to escape. Not one house was left undamaged, or one family left unharmed.

The reason for the reverberations of shock and horror were that such a thing had never happened before – death raining down from the air. The use of planes in war was only a few decades old and they had never been used on purely civilian targets. All over the world people realized that a new and even deadlier kind of war was beginning.

In Paris the Spanish painter, Pablo Picasso, was pacing the floors of his house.

"Pablo it's May Day," said his companion, Dora Maar. "We always go out in the streets and celebrate. Come on forget about the mural and let's go and enjoy ourselves."

"How can I enjoy myself?" yelled Picasso. "I have a sword hanging over me, a mural I have to paint and no subject. They want a mural for the Spanish Pavilion at the World Exposition, on the subject of technology and airplanes in particular. What do I know about ugly, silly planes? Not one idea that interests me comes into my head."

At that moment shouts came from the street,

"Down with the Fascist murderers!"

"Avenge Guernica!"

"Down with killers of women and children!"

Picasso and Dora ran to the window and saw angry crowds marching past.

"Guernica?" asked Dora, "What do they mean? What is it?"

"It is a town in the Basque country in Spain," replied the painter with a grim look on his face as he grabbed the unread newspaper on the table.

Opening it up he saw the headlines and began to shake: THE MARTYRDOM OF GUERNICA.

"Just listen to this," he said to Dora, and then he read out, "For three hours the German air fleet bombed the defenseless town. For three hours the German planes fired their machine guns on the women and children in the streets and in the fields, in all thousands of civilians were killed or injured. All of this in the name of civilization!"

They were both silent for a minute and tears ran down Picasso's face as he looked at the photograph of destruction and desolation on the front of the newspaper.

"My poor country" he wept.

"Why would they bomb this town?" demanded Dora. "Are there factories or soldiers there?"

"No," replied Picasso bitterly, "they just want to try out new methods of warfare and Guernica is a special place to the Basque people of that region. There is a tree there under which their leaders used to meet centuries ago to discuss events democratically. It is freedom and democracy they are bombing, and they are telling the world they don't care how many people they kill and who they are. This is what they call "total war" – no one gets left out, not even children."

"It's terrible, Pablo, terrible. What can we do?"

"I can paint a mural, that's what I can do. I have a subject now. I know just what to do with their wretched planes."

Picasso rushed out into the street and pushed his way through the huge crowds until he got to his studio. There he sat up all night making sketches for what was to become the most famous painting of the 20th Century – *Guernica.*

By dawn there was a series of sketches of terrified horses, a mother holding a dead baby, a maddened bull and bits of buildings, weapons and people flying about. Picasso imagined his own children being torn apart by war and that gave his work a passion and rage rarely seen.

Weeks later Picasso got to work on the actual painting. The picture was not a conventional war picture but showed the terrible fragmenting nature of war's destructiveness. In *Guernica,* everything seems to be flying apart, buildings, bodies, families, communities, civilization. All Pablo Picasso's fury went into the painting.

When it was finished it was taken to the Spanish

Pavilion at the World Exposition. When people looked at it they were shocked: no picture had previously expressed the savagery of war so intensely. Everyone had a strong reaction to *Guernica*. Some loathed it, most were incredibly moved.

"You know, Pablo," Dora told him, "when people look at your picture, they get emotional, they get angry, they want to stop this awful business."

"In that case I have succeeded," answered Picasso.

"Maybe we could send it round the world when the World Exposition is over," Dora suggested, "and spread the message about all the unnecessary pain and destruction."

"You really think my picture could do that?" asked the painter.

"I know it could," replied Dora, "Just look at the crowd. They can't drag themselves away from it."

So the painting of *Guernica* was taken all over Europe and the United States. Millions flocked to see it and were moved by the power of the message it conveyed. But there was one place Picasso refused to let it go, and that was his native Spain.

"This painting will be turned over to the government of Spain, the day freedom is restored to my poor country," declared Pablo Picasso.

When the Spanish Civil War ended, the Second World War began and many more cities were bombed like Guernica. However *Guernica* became the most famous picture of the 20th Century, and remains a very

155

powerful symbol of resistance to violence.

The painting was left in the Museum of Modern Art in New York.

When the dictator, General Franco died Spain finally became a democracy and in 1981, *Guernica* was finally returned to the Modern Art Museum in Madrid. Unfortunately, Picasso had died eight years earlier. To Spaniards the placing of the painting in Spain was a

very important symbol that they were finally a free country. It was a great moment in their lives.

Pablo Picasso not only produced one of the greatest war paintings ever, but also created a beautiful and charming symbol of peace – his white dove with an olive branch. Picasso helped to change the way we think about war and peace in a technological age.

Ann Jungman

Guernica (1937) by Pablo Picasso (1881–1973), Museo Nacional Centro de Arte Reina Sofía, Madrid.

My Heart Hurts

I don't understand.
Today you're kind
and care for me.
Yesterday your bombs
injured me.
I'm hurting bad
but my heart hurts more.

Nicola Smee

Hands

Hands.
Some hands are treacherous,
Holding guns,
Saluting, Waving.
Holding banners high.
Clasped round spoils of war,
Signing papers,
Grasps that slip in stealth from memory –
Leaving only the one poor, out-stretched palm
Reaching for pity's hard-bought bread,
Blanking the greedy circle of the camera's cold eye,
Clenching the sad shaft of a desperate spade,
Or hands invisible:
Those stumps, those blood-drenched shrouds
Where once were human
Hands.

Penny Dolan

Liberation

Twinkle, twinkle, little star
How I wonder what you are,
Up above our house so bright
Like a demon in the night.

I'm so scared of things that thump.
Scared to laugh, scared to jump.
I'm so scared of lights that shine.
Scared to walk, scared of mines.

They say that soon all this will cease.
They say that this will bring us peace.
You'll be liberated then, the soldiers said.
How I wonder, now my mother's dead.

Maggie Ling

Spoils Of War

Part One: The Jeweler

Once upon a time there was a jeweler.

He lived on his own in a small white house on the edge of a city. Six days a week he labored in his workshop, smelting precious metals and setting wonderful jewels to make beautiful things for the rich lords and ladies of the city. Although he worked with silver and gems he wasn't rich himself because every time he sold a piece of jewelry he spent all the money he made on even finer and more beautiful materials for his next piece of work. He had never married or had children and he never bought fine clothes or expensive food or luxurious furnishings for his house.

"My work is what is important," he told himself. "Someday I will make something so fine and so wonderful that it will touch the heart of everyone who sees it. Something that will be treasured for all time."

So he worked long hours in the dark workshop straining his eyes to do the delicate silverwork and his hands became knotted with the effort of keeping them steady and his back became bent from bending over the jewelled bracelets and combs and candlesticks he made for the rich people of the city.

But every seventh day he set aside his work and went out into the sunshine. He walked in the gardens of the city and admired the delicacy of the flowers, bending over to study the elegant construction of their petals and leaves. He walked past the houses of the poor people and watched the children running and playing in the dusty streets and shaded his eyes against the bright sunshine as he studied the grace and agility of their games as they ran and jumped and laughed together. He walked through the grand palaces and buildings of the city and studied the ornamented façades and the statues that seemed almost to live while made of stone. He walked all the way to the great temple at the center of the city and there he knelt and prayed, with his eyes shut as he thought of all he had seen.

"Everything You have made is so perfect, so flawless," he said silently. "Perhaps if You wish it, someday I might make something as worthy of being treasured."

And so he kept working and kept investing his profits into new materials and finally when he was an old man he made something he felt might at last be worthy. The smoothest clearest glass he could find was coated with the softest smoothest silver and set in a jewelled frame ornamented with flowers and leaves and the smiling faces of children. When he finally laid down his tools and turned to look at the elaborate jewelled mirror he was surprised to feel sad.

"This is it," he said to himself. "This is the finest thing I have made or will ever make." And straining his eyes he looked at his own lined face and his bent back and his gnarled hands in the smooth glass of the mirror.

"I have given my life to this work," he admitted. "But perhaps I have made something worthy of being treasured."

In that time it was the custom to send your finest fruit, if you were a farmer, or your finest cloth, if you were a weaver, or your finest work, if you were a craftsman to the King of that country. So the jeweler wrapped the fabulous mirror up in soft cloths to protect it and sent it to the palace as a gift for the King.

"I am old now, and likely to die soon," he told the messenger he paid with the last of his savings to carry it. "But I give my best work to the King and pray that he will find it worthy of being treasured."

Part Two: The King and the General

Fortunately the messenger was honest so the mirror was taken to the palace and there it remained for many years. But the King was a warlike and active man who spent most of his time riding to war and wasn't much interested in beautiful things, except as symbols of his power and wealth. So although the mirror hung on the wall of his stateroom he never really looked at the intricacy of the silverwork or the delicacy of the flowers or the shy faces of the children peering out through the leaves. He only looked at his own stern and proud face in the polished glass.

The King was eventually killed in one of his wars and was succeeded by his son, who was succeeded by his son, in the manner of Kings. And each one spent his time fighting wars and winning battles and accumulating more and more trophies and plunder so that the fabulous mirror was barely noticed amidst the gleaming splendor of the palace.

After many long years the army lost patience with fighting wars on behalf of their Kings. Although the palace was full of beautiful objects and gold and silver and jewels the people were poor and the soldiers not much better off. So the army rebelled and their finest General, who was a hero of the latest war, had the King and his family executed and stood on the steps of the palace while the people cheered and promised that he would end the wars against foreign powers and instead devote himself to the interests of the people.

The General kept his promise, after a fashion. He called the army back to the country and set them to guarding him and his advisers who had taken over the palace. He set them to watching the nobles of the city in case they should try to stage a revolt. And when the nobles had been executed or had fled, he set the army to watching the people. Because the General could never forget that he had led a rebellion and he feared that some day someone else would do likewise and overthrow him.

So when he looked at the fabulous mirror, he didn't recognize the flowers or the leaves because he spent all his time hiding in the palace. And he didn't see the children hiding in the silver branches, and if he had he would have thought they were spying on him. He only saw his own fierce and angry face in the polished glass.

This state of affairs went on for many years and although some of the people supported the General, many others were frightened of him. And the foreign nations the country had used to attack in the past flourished now that the army was fighting its own people instead of them. And the General in his palace became more and more paranoid that the people were plotting against him, and the people became more and more worried that the General might have any one of them executed.

Part Three: The Invaders

Finally one of the foreign countries decided to invade and tried to persuade the others to agree.

"Think of the poverty of the people!" the Invaders said. "We will help them against the brutal General."

"Are you sure you're not thinking of the rich treasures in the palace?" said the leaders of the other countries. "Won't the people suffer even more if you conquer them?"

But the Invaders insisted that they were in the right and they mounted an invasion force which swept into the General's country and attacked the army in every town and city and any people who were still loyal to the General and finally fought their way to the palace.

The General had fled with the last of his army, realizing that his fears had finally come to pass and frightened that he might be executed at the hands of the Invaders. The people had shuttered their windows and barred their doors and hidden themselves away, lest the Invaders think them supporters of the General and kill them as well. So when the soldiers of the invasion force came at last to the palace everything was quiet.

They hunted for the General in the empty rooms and kept their hands ready on their weapons but no one could be found anywhere. Eventually they came to the great rooms of state in which the generations of Kings and the General's supporters had entertained guests. There among the other ancient and priceless objects of the palace hung the fabulous mirror. Wide-eyed children stared from the ornamented frame, holding out flowers and garlands of leaves.

"Decadent, isn't it?" said a soldier, sitting back on the throne and kicking his feet up. "That General sure knew how to live though, didn't he?"

"Huh, call this treasure?" said one of his mates, sneering "What a lot of junk. Why it's nothing compared to the modern stuff we've got back home."

"Nothing for us to do here, anyway," said a third, grinding his cigarette into the intricately woven carpet stretched out on the floor. "Let's get back to base."

And as they walked out he glanced at himself in the mirror and made a jaunty salute, grinning at his own face reflected in the polished glass.

That night thieves came. And with no one to guard the palace they broke into the rooms and they looted the rich treasures and stripped the paintings from the walls and the carpets from the floors and the gold from the throne and smashed or set fire to everything they couldn't steal. One thief spotted the mirror hanging on the wall and lifted it down but it slipped from his fingers and struck the floor with a sharp crack, sending a slanting line across the smooth face of the glass.

The thief shrugged, looking at his own soot-blackened features warped and twisted by the polished glass. Then he began wrenching the jewels off the surround to be sold on the black market and the ornamented figures from the frame to be melted down for its silver the next morning.

Rhiannon Lassiter

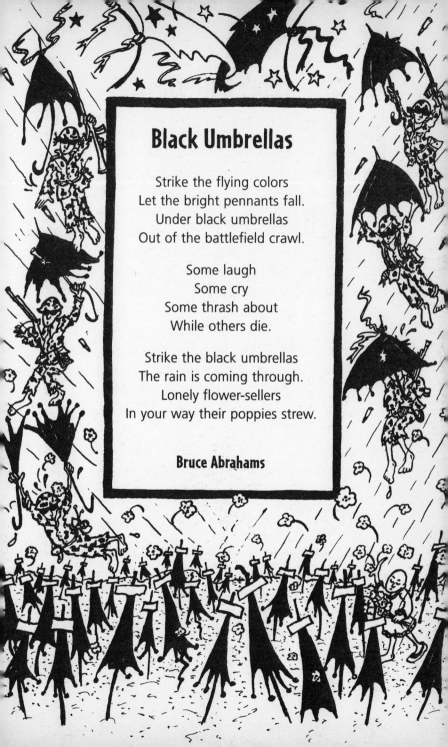

Black Umbrellas

Strike the flying colors
Let the bright pennants fall.
Under black umbrellas
Out of the battlefield crawl.

Some laugh
Some cry
Some thrash about
While others die.

Strike the black umbrellas
The rain is coming through.
Lonely flower-sellers
In your way their poppies strew.

Bruce Abrahams

Mira's Butterflies

Once upon a time there was a woman called Mira who had beautiful thoughts. They hovered round her head like rainbow-colored butterflies, and filled her house with light and warmth. Every day she fed them; and each day there were more of them.

Nearby, there lived a man named Hovik. He had greedy ugly thoughts that squatted like toads in the corner of the room, making his house dark and cold. Every day he fed them: every day they became stronger and more powerful, and his house grew darker than ever.

But Hovik didn't like having a dark house. When he saw that Mira's house was bright and warm, he wanted his house to be warm too. So he went to Mira and said, "Give me some of your butterflies so that my house will be as bright and warm as yours!"

Mira replied, "Yes, of course you can have some of my butterflies, but it won't do you any good unless you get rid of your toads. It's your toads that are making your house dark and cold!"

"My toads?" said Hovik in amazement.

"Yes! Turn your toads out of your house, and I'll give you some butterflies!"

Hovik pretended to agree; but he couldn't bear to lose his toads. He shut them up in his cellar, and told Mira that he had got rid of them.

Mira believed Hovik, and she gave him some butterflies. "Don't forget to feed them!" she said.

Hovik took the butterflies back home. At first, his house was bright and warm with the light that came from the butterflies, but he forgot to feed them any food. The dainty little butterflies grew weak and pale, and fluttered against the windows, longing to be free. Then the toads crept out of the cellar. They gobbled up the poor, weak butterflies with their long, slimy tongues, and Hovik's house was as dull and dark as ever.

Hovik sat looking at Mira's warm, bright house and his heart filled with envy. He went to Mira and said, "Those butterflies you gave me were weak, pitiful creatures. They've all died, and my house is still cold and dark. I don't want to live there any more. Let me come and live with you and your butterflies!"

Mira felt sorry for Hovik, and she let him move into her house. But the toads followed him. They hid under the furniture and waited until Mira had gone to bed. When she woke up, there were toads crawling all over her bedroom. All her butterflies had been eaten up, and her house was cold and damp.

"Get up, woman!" Hovik shouted at her. "The house is freezing! Hurry up and make some more butterflies!"

"I can't!" she cried. "The house is too cold!"

"Can't?" yelled Hovik. "You're useless aren't you!"

"It's your fault!" Mira cried. "I told you to get rid of those toads!"

"My fault? Oh no, it isn't! If your butterflies had

171

been a bit tougher, my toads would never have got them!"

"I'm not talking to you!" said Mira.

She sat in her corner, and Hovik sat in his. From time to time Mira tried to make more butterflies, but she was so full of angry, sulky thoughts that all she could make was toads. They each sat in their corners, sulking, and the more they sulked, the more the house filled up with toads. And because Mira couldn't forgive Hovik, she never made butterflies again.

Nicki Cornwell

The Dead Who Won't Stay Dead

The nightmare scenes that haunt his dreams
Repeat inside his head
The memories last, the bomb, the blast
And the dead who won't stay dead.

The deafening roar, the shaking floor,
The lucky ones who fled
The shattered glass, the fumes and gas
And the dead who won't stay dead.

The severed limbs, the blistered skin,
The wounds that poured and bled
The people killed are with him still
And the dead who won't stay dead.

Deep sleep is no escape
From the snapshots splattered red
The bomb goes on and on and on
A living nightmare never gone
There is no escaping from
The dead who won't stay dead.

Paul Cookson

Those Darn Flies!

There was this little old man living with his little old woman in a little old house on the edge of a wood.

They weren't rich; but they weren't so poor either that they couldn't afford a fine fat chicken for their dinner once in a while.

The old man killed it.

The old woman plucked it.

Together they collected wood for the fire, walking through the wild wood, there and back again.

The old man built up the fire and put the chicken on a spit to roast. The old woman laid the table and put out a loaf of homemade bread and a dish of freshly-churned butter.

Then they both sat down to wait for the chicken to cook. Oh, the smell of that chicken was something wonderful! And – oh! – the sizzling of the juices dripping onto the fire! And the sight of the meat slowly changing color from white to the palest shade of brown!

The old woman twiddled her thumbs and the old man sucked on his teeth.

"You know what we've forgotten?" she said suddenly.

"What's that?" he said, mouth watering, eyes fixed on that chicken slowly turning on its spit.

"Toothpicks!"

"Toothpicks?"

"Toothpicks for your teeth. If we don't have tooth-picks, you'll be searching with your tongue for bits of chicken-meat from between your teeth from now till Tuesday fortnight. And I'll have to listen to you!"

The little old man agreed, "We can't have that now, can we? We'd better go and fetch some. What about the chicken?"

"It'll probably cook the quicker if we're not watching it every minute."

"That's true. That's very true."

So off they went, in search of toothpicks. They were careful to lock the door behind them. They hid the key under the mat for fear of robbers.

Through the wild wood they went, searching for suitable bits of wood to use for toothpicks. Some were too thick and some were too thin. Some were too green and some were too dry. They were beginning to think they'd never find any that were just right when they met a likely lad strolling along the woodland path.

"Good-day to you!" says he. "And where are you two off to, this fine day?"

"We're off to gather toothpicks."

"We've a fine fat chicken for dinner, but my

old man –"

"My old woman! She says –"

"What about your fine fat chicken?" says the likely lad.

"We've left it turning on the spit."

"It'll be cooked all the sooner if we're not watching it."

"But if you're not watching it – aren't you afraid some thief might come in and steal it while you're gone?"

"Oh no! We've locked the door."

"And hidden the key under the mat, the same as we always do."

"Then I'd say your chicken is safe enough," said the likely lad. "I'll tell you where you can find toothpicks. Just walk a little further along this path and you'll come to the place where the woodcutters have been working. You'll be able to take your pick of toothpicks."

"Thank you," said the little old man.

"My pleasure!" said the likely lad.

"Such a nice young man!" said the little old woman, watching him go.

They went on down the path. It was a long while till they came to the place where the woodcutters had been working. And longer still before they could make up their minds which slivers or splinters of wood would be best for toothpicks.

Meanwhile our likely lad sauntered on till he came

to the house at the edge of the wood — oh! The smell of that chicken! — found the key under the mat, let himself in and had himself a very fine meal of fresh-roasted chicken and homemade bread and butter. Then let himself out again, locked the door, slipped the key back under the mat and went on his way.

Back came the little old man and the little old woman with their toothpicks; found the key under the mat; let themselves in. But where was their fine fat chicken? Gone!

Nothing but a bony carcass lying on the table, with the flies crawling over it. Flies picking at the crumbs that were all that were left of the bread. Leaving their dirty footprints in the last of the butter.

"Those darn flies!" yelled the old man.

"They've eaten our dinner!"

Neither of them stopped to wonder how the flies could have managed to unhook the chicken from the spit and haul it to the table.

"I've always hated flies." The little old man picked up the poker.

"Nasty, dirty things. There's one of them!" cried the little old woman. "There on the window! Get him, before he escapes!"

Thwack! went the poker. Crash! went the window-pane.

"There he goes!" The old woman picked up her rolling pin. "Don't let him get away!"

Swish! went the rolling pin.

Thump, thwack, smash! went the butter dish, onto the floor in a thousand pieces.

"There's another!"

"Mind the butter!"

Too late. Crash, bang, wallop! Over he went.

"Hold still – he's there on your leg!"

Thump! Thwack!

"Ow! My leg. I think it's broken."

"If that fly hadn't moved –"

"Darn flies!"

"Stupid creatures!"

"Not that stupid. They've had our dinner. There's another of them. Get him!"

"Get him!"

Crash! Bang! Ziggerzang!

We heard the row a mile away. But none of us dared go in. We waited outside till everything went quiet. I opened the door and peeped round it. There wasn't a cup or a plate that wasn't smashed; not a stick of furniture that wasn't broken into matchwood; not a window-pane still in one piece. And in the middle of it all, the little old man and the little old woman lying more dead than alive.

"Those darn flies!" he groaned.

"Aye," she sobbed. "Look what they've done to us. Those darn flies!"

Retold from a Gypsy folktale by MAGGIE PEARSON

Free At Last

In a corner of the palace grounds there was a small enclosure where there lived a lion. Lions had been kept there for as long as anyone could remember. Indeed, the rulers of that country had always had lions in their palaces, to show what great men they were to hold captive such a fierce animal.

This old lion had lived in the same pen since he had been taken from the wild, sixteen years before. His mane had now lost its luster and his coat was dusty and dingy with age.

He passed his days lying in what shade he could find, preferring, if it was too hot, the dappled shadow of a gnarled and bent tamarind tree. From beneath this tree the lion could watch for the approach of the man who brought him meat. While he waited, he would listen idly to the chatter of the sparrows who flew through the bars to drink or bathe in the muddy water of a stone trough.

Mostly the sparrows gossiped of the weather or where the best seed was to be had but every so often they would talk about the deeds of men and then the lion would be more attentive. Although he had been born in the wild hills far from the city, the lion had spent so long in captivity that he'd forgotten all that was natural for his kind. He knew only the confines of his cage and what he'd learned by observing his captors, though he had never understood the ways of men.

One day the lion woke to a distant roar like thunder. Thinking that a storm was on its way, he asked the sparrows about it, for they always knew of such things.

"No," answered the sparrows, "there's no storm; this thunder is a thunder caused by men." They said no more about it but flew off to peck crumbs from the crusts that a baker threw them. The lion blinked away the flies from the corners of his eyes and waited for the man to bring him meat. But that day the man didn't come and the lion went hungry.

Over the next days, the thunderous noise became louder and louder and the ground began to shake. A dark cloud dimmed the sun and hung like a shroud over the city. Even the sparrows stopped their twittering. The baker no longer threw crusts for them and they had to search elsewhere for food.

Each day the lion had watched for the man in the

hope of a meal but the man hadn't come and the lion had gone hungry. Restless with anxiety and fear, he paced back and forth under the tamarind tree.

During the night of the fifth day, the sound grew so great that the lion became dizzy with the pain of it in his ears and the ground shook so violently that he was afraid to sit or stand.

But by the time the first rays of the morning sun had seeped under the dark cloud onto the higher walls of the palace, the roar of thunder had ended. The lion lay in the dirt, exhausted.

The sparrows came and chattered, much as they had always done, but the lion was too weary to pay them any attention. When they had gone, he struggled over to the trough for a drink and found that a hole had appeared in the crumbling wall of his enclosure. He scraped limply at the stones with his great paws and despite his weakness, succeeded in making the hole large enough to pass through.

The lion was bewildered by what he found beyond the walls of his cage, it was all so new and strange. But his hunger made him bold. Shuffling through the streets, he looked for the man who had brought him meat. The air was heavy with the scent of flesh and the lion was hopeful. Saliva dripped from the corners of his mouth into the grey dust of the roadway.

He turned a corner and saw a group of three men. They huddled together and the lion, with dull instinct, sensed they were afraid. But his hope of food was so strong that he ignored the feeling and padded silently towards them.

The old lion took three more steps before he felt the sharp pain of a bullet bursting his heart. Three times he was hit. His slack limbs crumpled under him and he slumped to the ground. And as the blinding light of death enveloped him, he wondered at the ways of men.

Mark Burgess

Gulf

For Bryan

I awake on the *Lyonesse*,
a friend's boat moored up for the night
south of Worcester, off the Severn,
ironically in the oil dock.
I watch a lone black-headed gull,
dipping and bobbing in water,
cleaning itself; ripples expand
outwards in the grey morning chill.

Last night we saw stark images
of cormorants, oil slicked, helpless,
sloppily clinging to their lives
in a war-blackened foreign land.
We warmed our toes before the red
glow of the boat's coal burning stove,
helped by some glasses of whiskey
and good if stunned conversation.

Old friends such as we are, we find
there is no gulf between us worth
fighting over but oil tyrants
threaten even simple pleasures.
Perhaps we might be better off
without Saddam, without a Bush,
Mercutio's words come round again:
"A plague on both your houses."

Simon Fletcher

On The Beach At Cambridge

I am assistant to the Regional Commissioner
At Block E, Brooklands Avenue,
Communications Center for Region 4,
Which used to be East Anglia.

I published several poems as a young man
But later found I could not meet my own high standards
So tore up all my poems and stopped writing.
(I stopped painting at eight and singing at five.)
I was seconded to Block E
From the Ministry for the Environment.

Since there are no established poets available
I have come out here in my MPC
(Maximum Protective Clothing),
To dictate some sort of poem or word-picture
Into a miniature cassette recorder.

When I first stepped out of Block E on to this beach
I could not record any words at all,
So I chewed two of the orange-flavored pills
They give us for morale, switched on my Sony
And recorded this:

I am standing on the beach at Cambridge.
I can see a group in their MPC
Pushing Hoover-like and Ewbank-like machines
Through masses of black ashes.
The taller men are soldiers or police,
The others, scientific supervisors.

This group moves slowly across what seems
Like an endless car park with no cars at all.

I think that, in one moment,
All the books in Cambridge
Leapt off their shelves,
Spread their wings
And became white flames
And then black ash.
And I am standing on the beach at Cambridge.

You're a poet, said the Regional Commissioner,
Go out and describe that lot.

The University Library – a little hill of brick-dust.
King's College Chapel – a dune of stone-dust.
The sea is coming closer and closer.

The clouds are edged with green,
Sagging low under some terrible weight.
They move more rapidly than usual.

Some younger women with important jobs
Were admitted to Block E
But my wife was a teacher in her forties.
We talked it over
When the nature of the crisis became apparent.
We agreed somebody had to carry on.
That day I kissed her goodbye as I did every day
At the door of our house in Chesterton Road.
I kissed my son and my daughter goodbye.
I drove to Block E beside Hobson's Brook.

I felt like a piece of paper
Being torn in half.

And I am standing on the beach at Cambridge.
Some of the men in their MPC
Are sitting on the ground in the black ashes.
One is holding his head in both his hands.

I was forty-two three weeks ago.
My children painted me
Bright-colored cards with poems for my birthday.
I stuck them with Blu-Tack on the kitchen door.
I can remember the colors.

But in one moment all the children in Cambridge
Spread their wings
And became white flames
And then black ash.

And the children of America, I suppose.
And the children of Russia. I suppose.

And I am standing on the beach at Cambridge
And I am watching the broad black ocean tide
Bearing on its shoulders its burden of black ashes.

And I am listening to the last words of the sea
As it beats its head against the dying land.

Cambridge, March 1981
Adrian Mitchell

When the War Ends

When the war ends, will my father come back?
When the war ends, will my brother work again?
When the war ends, will my mother smile again?
When the war ends, will my grandmother laugh again?
When the war ends, will my little sister play again?
When the war ends, will my school start again?
When the war ends, will there be peace?

Wendy Blaxland

After The Bombing

The bombing began at night.
A long high whine! Boom! A flash!
Mother and I cowered in the corner,
holding on tight, but nothing
stopped our trembling.
Another whine! Boom! Flash!
More booms! More flashes!
Would the bombing ever stop?

With the dawn,
at last, it grew still.
Mother and I went up to our roof.
All around smoke curled from the ground.
People rushed on the streets,
pushing carts of chairs, beds, tables.
Without walls, the buildings looked like skeletons.
I had to look away.

That's when I saw the sky
bright and blue
with the sun shining
just like it had shone the day before
when there was no smoke,
when people had no need for carts,
when the buildings weren't broken.
And off in the distance,
I heard a bird singing.

Ann Whitford Paul

Peace

I had imagined Peace a woman
tall and cold, marble-refined
slender hands held in elegant lap
an expression of uncompromised calm

Or I had seen Peace an angel, with mighty wings
spread behind a halo of straw-colored curls
thick white robe to long thin feet
brandishing a flaming sword

So when Peace skulked in, wolf-thin and twitching
his ill-fitting suit stiff with mud and blood and centuries
    of dust
I stepped back, surprised. Closed my eyes
refusing to see his outstretched hand
missing finger and badly-bitten black nails

Sandra Guy

The world we made

A Mother's War Song

Little one,
Things will be better now,
The monsters have gone.

They've picked them off
One by one.

By bomb, by gun.

Little one,
Things will be better now,
Corruption has gone.

The Evil leader,
Torn from his place,
Ripped and dragged from the human race,
His statue toppled in to dust

Defiant, demonic
Tyranny crushed.

Oh yes, things will be better now
You wait and see
Good food, good times for you and me.

A happy house
A peaceful place
Books to read
Streets safe.

Money will flow like thick black oil
Coiling like a viper in the sand
Feeding our land.

Little one
But it doesn't matter,
All I've said,
For little one,
You are dead.

Kathryn White

Crèche

You should be playing with dolls
and teaching them how to sit straight
You should be playing with dolls
and tucking them in when it's late

You should be counting the clouds
and squelching the mud through your toes
You should be counting the clouds
and avoiding blowing your nose

You should be grazing your knee
by running through fields far too fast
You should be grazing your knee
and squealing at bugs that creep past

You should be flying a kite
and when it breaks getting vexed
You should be flying a kite
then asking, "What to do next?"

You should be playing with dolls
my frail lamb of unblemished fleece
You should be playing with dolls
You should be sleeping in peace.

Stewart Henderson

Dear Tallou

Dear Tallou,

I was just seven when I left our small, beautiful village Potamia without having a chance to say goodbye to you.

We were Greeks and Turks living together peacefully, sharing the differences of our cultures and religions respectfully until that hot summer day in 1964. The war suddenly and unexpectedly broke down to our village like a storm.

I was shocked when they told me that Greeks were our enemies. You were Greek, my close neighbor and my best friend. Don't worry; I have never believed them. I knew that they were mistaken. You were not my enemy, you were always my friend. You took care of me and loved me like my mother did.

Do you remember the song you used to sing me in Turkish? I have never forgotten it. Even after decades, I remember the sweet tone of your voice, when singing:

You're Aysel
You're beautiful
You're sweet like a candy
You're clever and naughty
You're Aysel
And I love you.

I sang this song to my daughters for many years. I also made up stories for them about us. Their favorite stories were the ones which started as follows:

"Once upon a time there was a beautiful and small village, Potamia, on a big island called Cyprus. A tall, beautiful young woman was living in that village. Her name was Tallou. Tallou's best friend was a little girl. The little girl used to call Tallou, *woman in black.* Because she always wore black dresses..."

I promised my daughters, that one day, I would take them to Potamia to meet Tallou, my best friend of my childhood.

Now that the borders are free to pass, now that I have the chance to keep my promise to my children, it just wasn't fair to hear that you are there no more. I know you were waiting for me all these years, and longing to see the little girl Aysel, in my daughters.

How can the years have passed so quickly? Why was it your time to pass away? Everything about you is in my heart and, believe me, there are no borders in my heart.

Now I am in Istanbul, but I promise I'll come to Cyprus as soon as possible to visit your grave with my daughters and bring you your favorite flowers, pink roses. Rest in peace.

With all my love,
Your little friend, Aysel

Aysel Gurmen

The Hair Ribbon

I brushed my daughter's silky hair today, but I couldn't see to tie a neat bow. "Silly mommy!" she scolded as my fingers fumbled. My eyes glittered with unshed tears. I thought about the children who would be killed today, and the mothers who would cry. Children just like Eleanor, who loved to run, and skip, and sing tuneless songs as they played. And mothers like me.

I saw, for one terrible moment, our house in ruins. Toys scattered, photographs broken. I saw myself weeping in the rubble over a small broken bundle.

I held her tight, breathing in her warm baby fragrance until she wriggled free to play with a more aloof playmate, the indifferent cat.

Later, I sat with coffee and a biscuit in my sunny living room, watching the television. A woman cried over her wounded child. Bombs had hit a market, as people shopped. Scraps of daily life lay in the ruins. A string shopping bag, a shredded newspaper, and a hair ribbon.

Lynn Huggins-Cooper

One Of Ours

For the unborn child and its mother, killed in
a Baghdad market, March 26th, 2003

Were you sleeping
In your cradle of skin and bone
When the world went deaf?

Was your mother
Buying onions and tomatoes
All there was left?

"It wasn't one of ours," the generals said.
They were wrong, or they lied.

Was your father
With his other sons and daughters
Or were you the first?

Did you wake up
And hear the muffled thud
When the world burst?

"It wasn't one of ours," the generals said.
They were wrong, or they lied.

It is never "one of theirs,"
Each bomb, each mine, each child.
We are the ones responsible.
It is always one of ours.

Mary Hoffman

Three

"Not bad, eh? All those planes and bombs
and they only killed three,"
says he
watching TV
in the safety of our country on the other side.

"What if they were our three?"
I ask.
I look at our boys
in their party hats
with chocolate caked faces
and a kite in their hands,
the tail streaming
like the colored streamers from our roof.
I look up – see now the yellow flash in the sky
and wonder which child's eyes
see hornets fly by
that don't bring birthday joy.

"What if they were our boys
who died. The three?"
He throws the beer can
and scowls at me.
"Don't be so bleedin' stupid!"
says he.

Leah Aplin

"THREE" © Sybille Sterk
2003

Lost and Found

In a flowery city in a faraway country, a baby was lying in a gutter. He was dirty, covered in sores, and so thin that his rib-bones pushed against his skin. He was hungry. He'd nearly stopped bothering to cry. Nobody took any notice of him. Babies were often abandoned on the street. Older children lived in cardboard boxes, and scratched about on rubbish dumps like chickens.

The night was noisy with bombs being dropped onto the villages outside the city. People were hurrying to get home before the curfew. A policeman on a bicycle heard the baby whimper. He picked the little boy up, took him to the nearest orphanage. It was called *Hoi Duc Anh*, which means "Society for the Protection of Infants." He left him in the office on a wicker chair.

Later, the boy-baby was wrapped in a piece of cloth for a diaper and laid in a cot. He stayed there, day and night, for several years. Twice a day he was fed. Once a day he was carried outside to the yard and hosed with water alongside the other unwanted babies, toddlers and children. As he grew up into a boy, he had a mat on the floor.

Some days, mothers or aunties or grannies came to the Hoi Duc Anh looking for their lost children. But in six years, nobody came looking for this child. He was given the name Nguyen Thanh Sang. Nobody knows now who gave it to him. Perhaps one of the women who worked in the orphanage.

Nguyen Thanh Sang had no toys, no books, no television, no chocolate, no aunties visiting, no school to go to. He smiled but he didn't learn to speak. One day when he was about five or six, some of the orphanage helpers gave him a red wooden brick and tried to teach him to walk.

When the fighting and the bombing was nearly over, Nguyen Thanh Sang was taken on a bus with 99 other children that nobody could agree what to do with. They loaded them onto a plane to Kuala Lumpur where the plane re-fuelled, then flew on to Britain. Nobody wanted them there either, except for the youngest, if they were pretty, and girls.

Most of the children had lots of disabilities. Nguyen Thanh Sang couldn't hear very well because of the bombs. He couldn't walk very well because of lying in a cot for so long, and not having had enough to eat, and he couldn't speak, but he grinned at anybody who looked at him. This was scary because he had so many black and missing teeth.

Nobody ever asked him what he wanted. He was taken with 19 other children from the faraway city to another orphanage. He stayed there for five years.
Then, one Sunday in Spring, I met him. And he came to live with me. He called me Mom. I called him Sang. I am still his mom. He is still my son, Sang.

Sang is now a grown-up man. But inside sometimes, he is still a frightened, confused, lost boy that nobody knew what to do with. Most of the time, however, he is happy. On Mondays, he plays five-a-side soccer. On Saturdays, he works in a café next to a cathedral and makes sandwiches and serves tea to visitors. Twice a year, he goes to the Blood Donation Center and gives some of his blood to be used for sick people.

Nobody knows his real birth date, not even what year he was born. But we do know the date that he came to live in my family. So, on the 21st anniversary of that date, we had a big celebration. Lots of food, cakes, soda drinks, champagne, laughing and music. People brought him cards and presents. People sang to him, and cheered him.

When the speeches and praises were over, Sang himself said in a quiet voice, "I make a speech too."

He is shy, can't always remember numbers or words, and can't talk clearly. But he stood up in front of a big crowd of friends and relations, and this is what he said: "Thank you for coming to this party. I am glad you came. I like the presents you bring me. I like my family here. And now one thing. I am thinking about the other children who come on the plane from Vietnam with me to this country. And I want us all to think about them. Some of them still quite sad, in children's home. One of them, Kim Yen, she has died. The others, some of them still there. We'll think of them."

Then he began to weep. And his big sister wept with him. And they held each other tight in their arms. And some of the rest of us wept too.

Sang's nephew, who is called Nguyen after his uncle's first name, said, "Why are all the grown-ups crying?"

I said, "We're crying because we're so happy and proud that Uncle Sang is here and always reminds us to think about other people too."

The next day, a visitor to the café where Sang works, said to him, "What a lucky young lad you are to have found such a big family to adopt you!"

Lucky? Losing everything in the world, including his own country? No, we're the lucky ones, to have him here in the middle of our family.

Rachel Anderson

Dear Mr. President

April 23rd, 2003

Dear Mr. President,

When my dad came home he was different. Before he went he used to laugh and play football. Now he's angry all the time and he has bad dreams so he doesn't sleep at night. He walks round the house talking to himself and drinking. Yesterday he hit my mom then he cried. My mom says we are going to stay with Granny and Grandpa. Mom says they are going to take my dad away for his own good.

I saw a little boy on television who had been blown up. My dad thinks he did it.

My dad's lost his mind and his family. The little boy lost his arms and his mom and dad.

I saw you in the paper sitting in your garden, with your hands behind your head, laughing. You said you told your children you might lose your job.

When I leave school I'm going to be a politician.

from,
Danny.

Nichola McAuliffe

Peacetime

There's a bird at the end of the garden
Bashing something to death on the paving.
Above, in the tree,
The hanging basket of Lizzies,
Scarlet and cerise,
Glows phosphorescent in the grey shadow,
Swings,
Releases slow dropping petals
Hushed as dripping blood.
And the radio tells me,
As if I didn't know,
That it's the Anniversary
of Hiroshima
Today.

Liz Berry

Rainbows, Stars And Stripes

Marco watches the rainbow-colored flags dance on the balconies and flap in the windows on the Grand Canal, splashes of color that have never decorated Venice before. He holds his grandmother's hand as they ride the public boat to the fish market at the Rialto Bridge. He listens to the sounds of his town: Venetian voices rise and fall like the water lapping in the canal; glasses clink at the ristorante; the engine of the boat grinds as it pulls up to the stop.

"Nonna," says Marco. "Why are there so many rainbow flags?"

"They're symbols for peace," says Nonna. "They wave all over Italy, but there are plenty here in Venice. Did you learn in school, Marco, that Venice was once called La Serenissima, the Most Serene Republic? Do you know what serene means?"

Marco shakes his head. "Is it a color? Like green?"

Nonna smiles. "No, caro. It means peaceful."

Marco and Nonna step off the public boat and into the bustle of gondoliers and merchants nestled at the foot of the Rialto Bridge. They brush past a tourist wearing a floppy top hat adorned with stars and stripes like a slapstick Uncle Sam.

"And the red, white and blue flags we see on television?" asks Marco. "With the stars and the stripes?"

Nonna hesitates. "Those are American flags."

Marco points to the red, white and blue pattern on the tourist's hat: "Are they the colors for war?"

Cat Bauer

213

George Square

My seventy-seven year old father
put his reading glasses on
to help my mother do the buttons
on the back of her dress.
"What a pair the two of us are!"
my mother said, "Me with my sore wrist,
you with your bad eyes, your soft thumbs!"

And off they went, my two parents
to march against the war in Iraq
him with his plastic hips, her with her arthritis,
to congregate at George Square where the banners
waved at each other like old friends, flapping,
where they'd met for so many marches over their years,
for peace on earth, for pity's sake, for peace, for peace.

Jackie Kay

The Wall

Look at this photo and tell me, do you recognize the little girl? See the color of my hair? Yellow like courgette flowers! Yes, I know, it's brown now with wisps of gray. And my skin isn't smooth and velvety like tulip petals and baby cheeks, but marked by years of laughter and tears and wind and sun. But inside I'm still that little girl, growing up in Belgium, listening to war stories. Funny, isn't it, how the story I remember most is the one about a boy climbing a wall after the fighting was over. I read about him in *Le Soir*, the very day of this photo.

So many stories. So many wars. Yet no matter the war, they were always stories of bravery and cleverness. Oh, and there's Mia, our Flemish maid, standing beside me. She used to tell us children about hardship at such times. "You should be thankful for what you have on your plates!" she said, "During World War II our family often went without food unless my brother managed to sneak some across the border, from France. Once, when he put butter under his hat, he prayed it didn't drip down his face while the officials checked his identity! If they caught you," she said, "they shot you dead."

And there's Mia's boyfriend, Isvan. I liked him. He was a butcher with a funny accent. He told us he escaped the Hungarian Revolution when he was 16. "Forced to leave everything I knew and loved, or be killed," he said. "Sliced myself climbing barbed wire fences and traveled hundreds of kilometers without food or water. Avoided capture, looking for freedom in a new country."

My French mother, who was 14 in World War II, had plenty of war tales too. "You should be proud," she said, "your six uncles fought with the Résistance, a group of secret soldiers." She told us the German troops, enemies of France, occupied her house. "Zey showed mama where they would machine-gun us before moving out," she said, "over by the well, so they could dump our bodies into it." But my grandmother was a devout Catholic, and when the day came to die she asked for permission to go to church for one last prayer. "By the time we got back, the Germans had left."

Lots of war stories. I can't even count them. Yet somehow, the words "Berlin Wall" still send shivers down my spine. I can still see the boy. He was 18, like my brother.

They were stories that made me despise the enemy and pity the victim, but I was always eager for more. Stories that blinded me to the horror, as if I was a caterpillar only vaguely aware of motion outside my cocoon. I have often asked myself why this is so. Is it because the tellers were silent, telling of glory but hiding the gory, so as to forget? Is it because the dead can't talk? Or is it because I was a lucky girl, privileged never to see war at my doorstep?

The grown-ups said World War II would end all

wars. I was glad to know everyone preferred peace. Then, when I believed the world had come to its senses, up came that wall, the Berlin Wall.

I remember the day clearly. I was sitting at the kitchen table, looking out towards the *Bois de la Cambre*, eating *goûter* – thick slices of crusty bread with chocolate spread – thinking about my homework. Madame Grenier had asked us to write a composition on any subject and to illustrate it with newspaper clippings. Long before I could read, I used to look through the papers and ask my father to explain pictures that caught my eye, like the one showing a Russian dog in a spaceship. But now that I was ten and could read, I'd seen the headlines: they were all about this Berlin Wall. And I knew what I must write.

Le Soir called it the beginning of the Cold War. So war wasn't over after all? Why did grown-ups lie but teach us not to? I peered at the black and white photos, which showed hundreds of people jumping, climbing, crying, and pleading with armed guards. And there was the wall. And there was the boy.

The Berlin Wall was built one Saturday night, in August, while East Germans lay sound asleep. Its purpose was to imprison inhabitants who hadn't done anything wrong, but who often left the East to go to the West because life was easier and more fun there. That night, troops put up barricades, tore up streets (not even sparing cemeteries) and completely sealed off the border, instantly separating children from parents, husbands from wives, sisters from brothers, and lovers from their sweethearts. When the East Germans awoke on Sunday morning, they discovered they could no longer cross over to the West. In desperation they tried all sorts of tricks: Two families sewed scraps of cloth together and drifted over the wall in a balloon; others jumped from upper floors of nearby buildings; others dug tunnels. Some escaped, but many died in the process or were caught and punished.

At first the Berlin Wall was little more than barbed-wire fencing with guard posts, but each phase of the building meant more and more reinforcement. By the final stage, when I'd turned 23, the wall was mostly concrete, stood about 12 feet high, and was nearly 100 miles long. It was protected by booby traps, floodlights, barbed wire, and armed guards who didn't hesitate to shoot those that dared try to escape.

The boy's name was Peter, I remember. He was just one of many victims shot while seeking freedom. *Le Soir* said the soldiers left him to bleed to death, right there where he fell by the foot of the Berlin Wall. When the Cold War ended, and the wall finally came down after 28 years of pain and suffering, I longed for a chunk of it. But I was too far away, somewhere up a river in Africa, facing yet another war.

Poupette Smith

For Carlos: A Letter From Your Father

I have never forgetten my tenth birthday. All my other childhood birthdays are lost somewhere in the mists of memory, blurred by their sameness perhaps, the excitement of anticipation, the brief rapture of opening presents and then the inevitable disappointment because birthdays like Christmases were always so quickly over. Not so my tenth.

It is not only because of the gleaming silver bike my mother gave me that I remember it so well. I tried it out at once, in my pajamas. In an ecstasy of joy and pride I rode it round and round the block, hoping all my friends would be up early and watching out of their windows, admiring, and seething with envy too. But even my memory of that has diminished over the years. It was when I came home, puffed out and glowing, and sat down for breakfast, that my mother gave me something else too. It is this second gift that I have never forgotten. I can't honestly remember what happened to my beautiful bike. Either it rusted away at the back of the garage when I grew out of it, or it was thrown away. I don't know. I do know that I still have this second gift, which I have never grown out of and never will.

She put down beside me on the kitchen table what looked at first like an ordinary birthday card. She didn't say who it was from but I could see that there was something about this card that troubled her deeply.

"Who's it from?" I asked her. I wasn't that interested at first - after all birthday cards were never as intriguing as presents. She didn't answer me. I picked up the envelope. There, written in handwriting I did not know was my answer, "For Carlos, a letter from your Father."

The envelope had clearly been folded, and was very dirty and was torn in one corner. The word "Father" was smeared and only just legible. I looked up and saw my mother's eyes filled with tears. I knew instantly she wanted me to ask no more questions. She simply said, "He wanted me to keep it for you, until your tenth birthday." So I opened the letter and read.

★   ★   ★

Dearest Carlos,

I want to wish you first of all a very happy 10th birthday. How I should love to be with you on this special day. Maybe we could have gone riding together as I once did with my father on my birthday. Was it my tenth? I can't remember. I do remember we rode all day and picnicked on a high hill where the wind breathed through the long grass. I thought I could see for ever from that hill. Or maybe we could have gone to a soccer match and howled together at the referee and leaped up and down when we scored.

But then maybe you don't like horses or soccer. Why should you have grown up like me? You are a different person, but with a little of me inside you.

That's all. I do know that your mother and I would have sung "Happy Birthday" to you and watched your eyes light up when you opened your presents, as you blew out the candles on your cake.

So all I have to give, all I can offer is this letter, a letter I hope you will never have to read, for if you are reading it now it means that I am not with you, and have never been with you, that I died ten years ago in some stupid, stupid war that killed me and many, many others, and like all wars did no one any good.

Dying, Carlos, as you know, comes to each of us. Strangely, I am not afraid, not as much as I have been. I think maybe that love has conquered my fear. I am filled with so much love for you, and such a sadness too, a sadness I pray you will never have to know. It is the thought of losing you before I even get to know you that saddens me so. If I die in this terrible place then we shall never meet, not properly, father to son. We shall never talk. For a father to be parted from his son is always a terrible thing, yet if it has to be, then in a way I would rather it was now, this way, this soon. To have known you, to have watched you grow and then to have lost you must surely be even worse. Or am I just telling myself that?

You will know me a little I suppose, perhaps from photographs. And your mother may well have told you something about me, of my childhood, how I grew up on the farm in Patagonia and was riding horses almost before I could walk. Maybe she told you of our first meeting when her car had a puncture and I stopped to change her tire for her. I am quite good at tinkering with motors – you have to be on a farm. But I took a lot longer to change that tire than I needed to – if you know what I mean. By the time I had finished I knew I loved her and wanted to spend my whole life with her. Later I learned that she went home afterwards and told her sister that she'd met this young man on the road who had nice eyes but who talked too much and was hopeless at changing tires. Anyway, much against the wishes of our families, who all said we were far too young, we got married six months later.

For a short while life seemed so sweet, so perfect. Then came my conscription papers and separation and the long months of military training. But I didn't mind that much because it was something we all had to do, because I knew it would soon be over. I had so much to look forward to, most of all the birth of you.

All the talk in the barracks was of war. I think we talked ourselves into this war – perhaps it is always like that.

I came home to see you just once, and now, only a few weeks later, I find myself sitting here in the Malvinas, high in the rocky hills above Stanley Town. Night is coming on and I am waiting for battle.

As I write this I am so cold I cannot feel my feet. I can hardly hold the pencil I am writing with. The British are coming. They know where we are. They have been bombarding us all day. We cannot see them, but we know they are out there somewhere. We expect them to attack tonight. All of us know in our hearts, though we do not say it, that this will be the last battle. In battle men die. I do not want to think of that, but it is difficult not to. The officers say we can win, that if we can hang on, reinforcements will soon be here. But we all know better. They have to say that, don't they?

I can see you now in my head, on the morning I left home three long months ago. When I looked down upon you that last time, cradled in your mother's arms I tried to picture you as a grown boy. I couldn't and I still can't. For me you are that sleeping child, yawning toothlessly, fists clenched, frowning through your milk-soaked dreams. But grow up you will, grow up you have, and now that you are old enough I want you to know me as I am now. I want to tell you myself how I came to be here, in this dreadful place, and how I died so far from home. I want to speak to you directly. At least you will know me a little because you can hear my voice in my writing. I am writing to you partly because it helps me. If I think of you I do not think of the battle ahead. I have already written to your mother. She will have read her letter ten years ago now. This is your letter Carlos, our hello you might call it, and our goodbye.

I had not thought it would end like this. Like all my comrades I believed what we were told, in what we saw on the television, in what we read in the papers. The Malvinas belonged to Argentina, and that much is true.

They had been stolen from us, they said. We would restore the honor of Argentina and take them back. Our flag would fly again over Stanley. It would be easy they told us. We would attack in force, overwhelm the British garrison in a few hours. There would be very little shooting. The Malvinas would be ours again, Argentinian, and then we could all go home. I was excited – we all were excited and proud too, proud that we were the ones chosen to do this for our country. It was all going to be so simple.

And it began so well. We came ashore in our landing craft. As we marched into Stanley we saw our flag already flying high over the town. The British marines in their green berets sat huddled by the roadside dejected, defeated. The war was over almost before it had begun. Or so we thought. We had won. The Malvinas were ours again. How the people back home would be cheering, I thought. What heroes we would be when we returned. How we laughed and sang and drank that first night. We did not feel the cold in the wind, not then.

In those early days on the Malvinas, in that first flush of victory, the islands looked to us like a paradise, a paradise regained. Our paradise. Argentinian.

Yet here I sit only a month or two later and we know that we are about to lose the last battle. The ships did not come. The supplies did not come. Instead the British came, their planes first, then their ships, then their soldiers. We did what we could, Carlos, but we were raw conscripts, poorly fed, poorly equipped, badly led and we were up against determined fighters. From the moment they sank the great battleship *Belgrano*, the pride of our navy, we knew it could only end one way. I saw men die, good men, my friends, men with wives and mothers and children.

I grew up fast in the terrible weeks that followed. I learned what I should already have understood, that in wars people really do kill one another. I did not hate those I have killed and those who try to kill me do not hate me either. We are like puppets doing a dance of death, our masters pulling the strings, watched by the world on television. What they don't know is that the puppets are made of flesh, not wood. War, Carlos, has only one result.

When I heard the British had landed at San Carlos Bay I thought of you, and I prayed in the church in Stanley that I would be spared to see you again. They had no candles there. So I went out and bought a box of candles from the store and then I came back and lit them and prayed for me, for you, for your mother. An old lady in a scarf was kneeling at prayer. I saw her watching me as I came away. Her eyes met mine and she tried to smile. My English is not that good but I remember her words. They echo still in my head.

"This is not the way," she said. "It is wrong, wrong."

"Yes" I replied, and left her there.

That was a few days ago now. Since then we have been stuck up here on these freezing hills above Stanley

Town, digging in and waiting for the British who come closer every day. And the bitter wind, from which we cannot hide, chills us to the bone, sapping the last of our strength and most of our courage too. What courage we have left we shall fight with, but courage will not be enough.

I must finish now. I must fold you away in an envelope and face whatever I must face. As you grew up, you may not have had a father, but I promise you, you have always had a father's love.

Goodbye dearest Carlos. And God bless.

Papa

Michael Morpurgo

War Games

For my Dad, with love

My father made his hand a gun
And pointed it at me.
One finger points, the thumb outstretched,
Fold down the other three.

But playing war with my dad
Was different, you see,
He'd kiss his palm, then make the gun,
Then fire, wounding me:

And I would die, shot through with love,
His kisses made me pain,
Shot through with love, the hurt would die,
But I would live again.

Mark Svendsen

Dad's Hat

I found it again just last week, this photograph. Dad's wearing that hat in it, the one he brought back from Burma. Remember? Heavy brown felt. One side of the rim's dead flat, the other's vertical. I'm sure we played with it when we were kids. I'm sure I remember how soft and heavy it was. I can nearly smell it. I can feel it dropping over my eyes when I put it on. I can hear him laughing and feel his fingers as he lifts it off me again. How old was I? Four? Five?

He looks so young, so calm, so glad to be back home again. It must have been taken in '46, when he came home with all of the Forgotten Army.

Everybody's there, aunts and uncles, all of them in uniform: Jan and Mona in their Land Girl dungarees; George in his Home Guard drill; Amos with his collar and tie and his would-be scholar's specs; Alban with his corporal's stripes. And Charlie's there, the uncle that none of us would ever know. They're in the garden at Ell Dene Crescent, where we'd all play once we'd come into the world. All those games of ours: bombing Berlin, shooting the Germans, bayoneting the Japanese...

I've been looking at it closely. I think I'm looking for a sign of what he's been through: some scars on his skin, some hint of nightmares in his eyes. But there's nothing visible. Just calmness, relaxation, relief. I even caught myself looking for a sense of dread for what's to come. But there'd be none of that, would there? He's looking to a bright future, like all of them. The war's gone, a great new time is on its way. Remember how he used to say we were so privileged? "You can do anything," he used to say. "Anything. You won't be hauled out of your life and sent to war."

Just look at him. Hardly more than a boy. Awful to think he'd only last another twenty years. Just twenty years between the war's end and the coming of his cancer. Soon he'd be married, he'd be working at George Angus, and pretty soon Colin would be born, and then the rest of us, into a peaceful world. We'd play in Felling's gardens, we'd have our orange juice and malt and our injections. We'd go to grammar schools and grow our hair and go to universities and lie on sofas reading and march against The Bomb and protest about Vietnam. He'd see hardly any of this. But his words would stay with us, "Go on. You can do anything. Anything."

Twenty years. They called them years of peace, but Mam said the war must have continued, somewhere deep inside him. She said it was the effects of war that took him from us in the end. Can it be true? Can war, that thing of bombs and planes and noise and armies and great battles that reach all around the world, also be something tiny, something silent, something that can creep unseen into the cells of a handsome young man and bring him down as surely as any bullet? Who can know? He looks so well, but who can see what's happening, somewhere deep inside? Poor lovely man. There he is, gazing out at me through these more-than-fifty years. I touch the image of his face. I miss him so. Hello, Dad.

I think of what might have happened afterwards, once the photograph had been taken. I picture him leaving his brothers and sisters in the garden. He walks beneath the trees on Chilside Road and Rectory Road. The skylarks hang in the air and sing and sing. He goes to Mam's house. They whisper together in her garden. She lifts the hat from his head and tries it on and feels the softness and heaviness of it as it drops across her eyes. He laughs as he lifts it from her. He kisses her. We'll have a lovely life, he whispers, you and me and all the little ones to come.

What happened to that hat? Who saw it last? I'm sure that someone somewhere once told us where it is, or where it might be, or where we might at least consider searching. If only I could remember those rumors. I've been searching and searching for it, but I expect that, like him, it won't turn up again.

David Almond

Sonnet Against War

I am a woman, I hold the child,
Under the breastbone, close to the heart;
I wash the linens, crusty and soiled,
I pile dead bodies onto the cart.
I am a woman, I feed the soldiers,
Hungry and hopeless, milk from my breast;
I rock the cradles, I move the boulders,
I am a woman, I get no rest.

I am a woman, I am the witness,
I cry to heaven; if I'm not heard.
I write the pamphlets, I make the impress,
I am the woman, I know the word.
Better be careful, men who make war,
We women know what we're fighting for.

Jane Yolen

Love Poem
(Wednesday morning, March 19th, 2003)

she cuts off her hair
she shaves her head
daubs ashes on her face

as statesman and politician
heap disgrace upon disgrace

she digs up earth
plants rye, plants wheat
feeds thousands with her bread

weeps for the politicians
juggling bombs about her head

but the thousands she fed
the thousands unborn
are smashed, violated, dead

she cuts off her hair
she shaves her head
feeds thousands with her bread

plants daffodils,
plants rye, plants wheat
writes a poem for a child she fed.

Joan Poulson

I Would Like To Think

I would like to think
that because your hands
are smoother than mine
and because your hands are smaller
and softer that you will not
pick up a stone
except to skip it across the river
into which you will soon dive

I would like to think that
knowing what the old have done
you will remember
never to act your age
never to think
that there could ever be a reason
to pick up a gun

I hope you would
like to think that too

Chris Mansell

Seeds of hope

13 Ways Of Looking At Peace

"It is an historic milestone of immense proportions. It has never happened before, never in human history, and it is happening now, every day, every hour, waging peace through a global conversation." paraphrased from a March, 2003 speech by Dr. Robert Muller, former Assistant Secretary General of the United Nations, now Chancellor Emeritus of the University of Peace in Costa Rica.

Passing cherry blossoms in Washington, DC,
a cab driver teaches the chorus of a peace song

to the woman with freckled arms from Malibu,
who gives him a big tip and runs up the hotel stairs
two at a time
to write a letter to the editor

who tilts back in his squeaky chair and reads it
by the light from his arched window and then publishes
her letter

which my uncle Chucky reads in Anchorage,
inspiring him to write a peace poem on the blackboard

which Ruthie reads, whispering to herself twice,
then copies down on notebook paper,
folds, puts in her back pocket,
and when she gets home, smoothes out and emails

to Renee in Sweden
who !!!!loves!!!! it and immediately !!!!forwards!!!! it
to Finley in Hong Kong, Alice in New York,
Fadi in Beirut, Lyra in Moscow,

and Bruce near Netanya
who reads it at a candlelight vigil by the beach

which is broadcast to Saralee in Buenos Aires
(petting Spartacus, who is shedding all over the bed),

who phones Ross, telling him to turn on the radio,
good old Ross, who is eating soft vanilla ice cream
as he listens,
Ross, who takes out a napkin and his guitar,
and turns it into a song

"This," Dr. Muller says, *"is a miracle. This is what waging peace looks like."*

April Halprin Wayland

Family Photo, '45

Peace, for me, is a black and white photo,
Chubby little girl in a paper crown.
Frowning at the sun, she stands on a chair,
In a street that is full of chairs, and of children,
Food on the tables, Bakelite beakers
With red and gleaming victory "V"s.
And she is embraced, safely secure,
Within her brother's broken arm.

Susie Jenkin-Pearce

Away from War

That a dog might always
be barking at late afternoon sun
and the kids on bikes
yelling out "See ya"
and the bees windmilling
the last of the rosemary pollen.

That the wind might be
skitching a tree branch
on the galvanized roof
and always but always,
the promise of tea, talk and night
just warmed by Your golden light.

Lorraine Marwood

The Quarrelsome Trees

The teacher told the children that they were going to plant trees in the school garden the next day. The children were excited since there would be no classes. How nice it would be, every child thought. They'd have so much fun!

When it was time to plant the trees, the teacher gave each child a young tree and explained how to plant it. As the children started to dig holes in the soil, two children started to quarrel.

"Give me that plant. It's mine." The children jostled and pushed each other.

"No, it's mine. The teacher gave it to me."

"Yours is an apple tree. I want it!"

"No it's not. It's peach!" shouted one child angrily.

"Mine is peach. Yours is apple!"

"No it's not!"

The children went on quarrelling. They always found something to fight over. So it wasn't unusual that they forgot what they were fighting for and started to argue over the place to dig.

"Go away, this is where I'll put my tree."

"I won't. This is exactly where I'll plant my tree."

"This is my place."

"No mine..."

They hurried to grab a piece of land, and each dug a hole nearly on top of the other's.

Finally all the trees were planted and watered. It was

time to go home.

Several years passed. The trees in the school garden grew into beautiful trees with delicious fruits. Except two. Which two? The ones that were planted by the two quarrelsome children... These trees had been behaving exactly like their planters...

"Go away, will you? You are shielding my sun."

"You fool! It's your own leaves that are blocking my light."

"I need the sun to grow! Why should I do that?"

"Because you are stupid!"

"You are stupid! Take away your branches. I'll suffocate!"

"You'll suffocate because you eat and drink too much!"

"You think so? I cannot move my roots even an inch!"

No birds, no caterpillars, no squirrels visited these trees. Not once did a butterfly touch their leaves. Nobody in the garden liked them and no one wanted to be their friend.

The two quarrelling trees withered more and more every day. The few leaves they had managed to grow, dropped; branches drooped and dried up. The headmaster of the school called a tree surgeon before it was too late.

The tree surgeon carefully examined the trees, nodded his head, and finally said:

"These trees have been planted thoughtlessly. They

are interfering with each other's freedom. So, they cannot spread their branches smoothly to benefit from the sunlight; their branches have tangled up into knots. Their roots are jumbled in the soil, and cannot move to reach food to grow. Sorry, there is nothing I can do. They have blocked each other's freedom."

The trees were very ashamed about what they heard. They stopped quarrelling and looked at each other.

"What do we do now?"

"I don't want to keep on quarrelling."

"I don't either. It takes my energy away."

"Is it too late? Too late to be friends?"

"Do you think we can live long enough to be friends?"

A bird nesting on the branch of one of the other trees in the garden heard what the withering trees said. It flew towards them and perched on a weak branch for the first time.

"If you are friends, we will be friends too. Don't you know that friends help each other?"

The bird called all the other birds to help. They each took one branch in their beaks and pulled, leaving the branches free to breathe and enjoy the sunshine.

Then the worms offered to help. They all spread around the knots and freed the roots.

For the first time in years, the trees stretched freely, spread their branches wide, and sent out roots to far away places they've never been.

They looked at each other.

"Oh, I'd never noticed. You are such a beautiful tree."

"You are too."

The birds chirped and swung on the branches, the caterpillars roamed around the leaves to find a suitable home, worms danced around the roots, butterflies spread their colors on the flowers.

Peace reigned in the garden, touching them all like a miracle.

Aytul Akal

Early Monday Morning

All around the world
the birds were singing
the salmon swam upstream to spawn
a crab scuttled sideways
on a lonesome beach
enjoying the crazy dance
a dog lazily wagged his tail
as he dozed under a
spreading oak tree
and two butterflies floated
on the warm east breeze
to show us all
how stupid we humans are.

Steven Herrick

Ruling The World

I should like to rule the world;
I think it's my turn now
I could make things so much better
and I'm going to tell you how:
I'd melt down all the guns and bombs
and all those evil things,
And turn them into bicycles
and carousels and swings.
Turn them into roller skates
and bongo drums and bells,
Make spinning tops and glockenspiels
from all the tanks and shells.
Fill the world with happy things
that make a happy noise;
Shout it all around the earth:
Don't make war, make toys!

Sandra Horn

Eco-Wolf And The War Pigs

In a beautiful valley beside a twisting stream, lived a wise and gentle creature called Eco-Wolf.

The valley was a peaceful place and the wild animals lived together like one happy family. From the hugest hairy bear to the tiniest baby bunny, it was wonderful how all the animals got along.

All the animals? No! Three fat piggies shared that valley, and they were not peaceful at all. They spent their time squealing and squabbling and bickering and boasting.

Eco-Wolf and the baby rabbits planted an apple tree for everyone to share, but the piggies got there first.

"Oink!" squealed the First Pig. "He's got three apples, so I'm taking four."

"Oink! Oink!" squealed the Second Pig. "He's got four apples, so I'm taking five!"

"Oink! Oink! Oink!" squealed the Third Pig. "I'm taking six apples and squashing yours on the floor."

Their behavior was DISGUSTING! It set a very bad example to the small animals of the valley.

"Listen, piggy brothers," said Eco-Wolf. "You're, like, spoiling the valley vibe. If you cannot live together, I will help build three houses of your own."

248

"Oink!" squealed the First Pig. "I want a straw house – with a lock on the door."

"Oink! Oink!" squealed the Second Pig. "I want a wooden house, with a fence all around. And a statue of me in the garden."

"Oink! Oink! Oink!" squealed the Third Pig. "I want a brick castle with lots of flag posts and a cannon on top."

Day and night, the selfish pigs jabbed and jeered. And the baby bunnies could not sleep in their beds.

"Like, huff and puff," sighed Eco-Wolf. "I don't dig these big bad pigs."

The War-Pigs began to collect horrible things to hurt each other and hid them in their houses –

"Oink!" squealed the First Pig. "You've got stinging nettles, so I will throw acorns."

"Oink! Oink!" squealed the Second Pig. "You're throwing acorns. I will throw fir cones."

"Oink! Oink! Oink!" squealed the Third Pig "You're throwing fir cones, so I will fire cow poo from my cannon."

As the acorn bombs flew, the whole valley began to shake. It made the baby bunnies cry.

Only Eco-Wolf was wise. He called a meeting of all the valley animals and the War Pigs were invited too.

"Like, huff and puff!" said Eco-Wolf. "You pigs should learn that we are ALL brother-sisters, man. This fighting is totally uncool."

"Oink!" squealed the First Pig. "Sometimes war is

necessary. I am fighting for you."

"Oink! Oink!" squealed the Second Pig. "They started it. And they keep laughing at my statue."

"Oink! Oink! Oink!" squealed the Third Pig. "I am trying to make the valley a safer place. Anyway, God is on my side."

Eco-Wolf was patient and Eco-Wolf was wise — "Let's talk it through like grown-ups, man."

But the War Pigs were not listening. They began pinching and punching and poking and soon they walked out of the meeting.

In the middle of the night, the First Pig and the Third Pig began to whisper:

"Oink!" squealed the First Pig. "I am only a small piggy and you are a big pig with God on your side. If I give you my fir cones we can fight together."

"Oink! Oink! Oink!" squealed the Third Pig.

"You can load my cannon and we'll blow that pig into pork scratchings!"

So the First Pig and the Third Pig joined together. The big pig stood in front, shouting and boasting and the little pig held onto his tail behind. Two pigs are stronger than one pig and soon they began to beat the Second Pig.

The war was more terrible than ever. The baby bunnies trembled with terror as acorns fell all around.

Eco-Wolf was in despair. "Hey, Piggy Brothers," he cried, "Let's behave in a CIVILIZED way. We can SHARE this beautiful valley."

But the War Pigs had lots of fir cones and stinging nettles and thought God was on their side.

"Oink!" squealed the First Pig. "Get out your gas masks. That pig is hiding deadly skunk juice and it sure smells bad."

"Oink! Oink!" squealed the Second Pig. "I have no skunks. The bad smell is you!"

"Oink! Oink! Oink!" squealed the Third Pig. "God is on our side and we've got Smart Bombs – load the cannon with PORCUPINES!"

Before long, the beautiful valley was a smoking mess. The poor animals were too frightened to collect apples from the tree or water from the stream. They became thirsty and hungry and afraid. The First Pig and the Third Pig knocked down the fence around the wooden house and pulled down the Second Pig's statue. "Victory!" they shouted, "Liberation! Oink! Oink! Oink!"

Then a terrible thing happened – one baby bunny, the tiniest bunny in the valley, ran outside to find her mummy. "Like, come back, tiny bunny!" called Eco-Wolf. But it was too late! A stray fir cone fell out of the sky and knocked the baby bunny flat.

Eco-Wolf ran outside and lifted the little creature in his arms. As he bandaged her head, tears ran out of his wise wolfie eyes.

"This makes me mad!" sobbed Eco-Wolf. "This makes me BALLISTIC! This makes me HUFF and PUFF! I'm going to give it to those porky pigs on the chinny-chin-chin!"

"Hooray!" shouted the animals. "We will come with you. Let's collect fir cones and stinging nettles and skunk poo and..."

"Like, cool it brother-sisters," said Eco-Wolf. "Let's LEARN from those pigs. Can't you see that war won't work? Lay down your fir cones. Lay down your skunk poo."

Eco-Wolf lifted the tiniest bunny onto his shoulders. Slowly he stepped into the noonday sun. He carried a sign: "Wolves Against War!" And the tiny bunny held a tiny sign: "Bunnies Against Bombs!"

The three pigs were wild with war fever. They had ruined their piggy houses and smashed their piggy statues and burned their piggy flags.

But Eco-Wolf was brave. He marched across the battlefield and stared straight into their porky eyes.

"LIKE HUFF AND PUFF, WE'VE HAD ENOUGH!" he shouted. "These are my brother-sisters you are bombing. You are squabbling like spoilt brats. It is time to be WISE!"

"Yes!" shouted the animals, creeping out of their holes. "There will be NO END to war, if we cannot be wise."

"Oink!" said the First Pig. "I AM the wisest War Pig."

"Oink! Oink!" squealed the Second Pig. "I am bigger than you, so I must be the wisest War Pig."

"Oink! Oink! Oink!" squealed the third pig. "I am bigger than both of you and I have God on my side, so I must be the wisest War Pig of all."

"Like, wait a minute," said Eco-Wolf. "Sometimes the SMALLEST person can be the wisest. There is a bunny here we can ALL learn from."

Everybody looked around. Eco-Wolf lifted the tiniest bunny off his shoulders and stood her on a tree stump.

"Oink! Oink! Oink!" squealed the War Pigs, "What can we learn from a baby?"

"Tell them, little lady," whispered Eco-Wolf.

In a tiny funny bunny voice the little rabbit began to speak –

"My mommy says fighting is bad, mister."

"YES!" shouted everybody. "Fighting is bad!"

"You hear that, piggies?" said Eco-Wolf. "Now pack your piggy bags and leave our lovely valley."

So the three War Pigs crept slowly away, battered and beaten and bruised. Oink! Oink! Oink! And I'm very pleased to tell you that they were never seen again.

Peace returned to the valley. From then on, whenever there was a decision to be made, all the animals would talk together. When they found it hard to share, they would ask the baby bunny for advice. "One apple each," she would say. "And NO FIGHTING!"

And Eco-Wolf picked up his guitar and sang to the stars: "In the words of Bob Marley, man... like, one love, one heart, let's live together and feel all right...."

Laurence Anholt

The Flag

In war too many die for me,
Yet of simple cloth I am born,
A soldier hoists me way up high,
Then lowers me when I am worn.

My suit is of many hues,
In places near and far,
Stripes of orange, green or blue,
Adorned with a wheel, or star.

These border-lines that man has made,
Can they cut the sky we see?
The air we breathe and the earth beneath,
Are they not totally free?

When birds fly through the blue above,
Does the sky not stay as one?
Then why point at our fellow man,
With the barrel of a gun?

Feel strong winds blow through your clothes,
Stand up straight and proud.
Hear trumpets blow the anthem notes,
As light appears from behind a cloud.

Gain strength from looking up at me,
Rise in peace and never lag,
But let others rise along with you,
For they too may love their flag.

Stephen Aitken

When People Pick Up Guns

When people pick up guns,
They pick up people.
When people pick up bullets,
They pick up lives.
When people aim their guns,
They aim at people.
When people shoot their bullets,
They shoot out lives.

When people go to war,
They blow up houses.
When people blow up houses,
They knock down homes.
And all the living people
In the houses
Are dead. Or dying. Leavings
Of skin and bone.

When people lay down guns,
They help up children.
When people lay down bullets,
They lift up life.
When people bomb with flower,
Seed and blossom,
Peace explodes, fruits and grows. War
Withers and dies.

When people throw out hate,
They bring in love.
When people imprison war,
They let peace free.
When people end the killing
To start a new
Beginning. We live! Live on,
Our children's children.

NO MORE WAR!

Gwen Grant

Give Peace A Chance.

It was early morning on April 10th, 1993 and South African politician, Mr. Chris Hani, had just entered his driveway after a quick trip to the local shop. He didn't notice the car slowing in the road behind him. Suddenly, gunshots rang out, and Hani slumped in the driveway. He was dead.

The news of the assassination of this dedicated and popular black leader quickly spread though South Africa. The country erupted in anger and fear.

Civil war seemed unavoidable.

It was a tragedy. For three years the country's leaders had been holding talks, trying to find a way to end the years of oppression and fighting. And now it seemed that the progress they had made might be lost.

On one side stood the nationalist government, led by President F.W. de Klerk. It had been in power for nearly 50 years. It believed that black people were inferior to whites, and had passed laws to make sure that black people could not live near whites, or go to the same schools, hospitals or doctors.

Black people were forced to leave their houses and sent to live far away from the cities. The best areas were kept only for white people. People of different races were not allowed to marry each other, or go to the same restaurants, cinemas or beaches. Even amenities like swimming pools and sports grounds, post offices and railway stations were strictly segregated.

But most iniquitous was the fact that people of color were not allowed to vote for the government. They had no legal way of changing these cruel and unjust laws. People who protested against these laws were viewed as enemies by the government. Many were imprisoned for years without ever getting a trial. They were tortured, forced into exile or banned from leaving their homes. Many died in mysterious circumstances.

On the other side stood the leaders of the African National Congress. They wanted all South Africans to be seen as equal. They wanted an end to racism and discrimination, and a fairly elected government in place. However, anyone found belonging to the ANC was arrested by the government. For many years, most of the leaders of the African National Congress had been imprisoned on Robben Island, a desolate rocky outcrop off the coast of Cape Town, from where there was no hope of escape. The most famous prisoner, Nelson Mandela, had spent 27 years in prison.

The armed wing of the ANC, known as *Umkhonto we Sizwe*, or the Spear of the Nation, operated from outside South Africa's borders. Its leaders believed that a violent revolution was the only way to overthrow the government.

But within the country one particular voice stood out, calling for justice and reconciliation. Archbishop Desmond Tutu was a small man, with a lion's heart. Time and time again, he stood in front of angry crowds, urging them not to take matters into their own hands, but to follow the ways of peace and forgiveness. Repeatedly he called on the government to stop oppressing his people. And he called on countries across the world to stop trading with South Africa and to stop playing against its sports teams until it had a democratic government in place.

The nationalist government feared and hated Archbishop Tutu, but they were too afraid to stop him. He had too much support across the world. His methods of peaceful resistance worked. The pressure on the South African government from the rest of the world increased. Initially it responded by making its laws more cruel and oppressive. But slowly the government realized that it could not hold on forever. The longer it oppressed the people, the angrier they became. The country was heading for a blood-bath.

Then, from inside his prison cell, Nelson Mandela sent a message to the government. "Let us talk," he said. "There must be a way to justice if we sit down together." At last, the government agreed. Nelson Mandela and other political prisoners were released from jail. The world watched with bated breath as the two sides sat down together and tried to work out a solution to the problem, one that would please everyone.

The whites were afraid that if the blacks came to power, they would seek revenge for their years of suffering. The blacks were afraid that the whites would not want to share power equally, or would try to trick them. "Give peace a chance," Archbishop Tutu and Nelson Mandela begged. "It is the only way to freedom."

The talks began. Chris Hani was one of the leaders who encouraged his people to find justice through negotiations, not through war. Things were going well, until the morning of April 10th, 1993. The two sides had finally found some common ground. And then Chris Hani was shot. His death was the last straw to those impatient with enduring pain and suffering. It seemed as though all chances of peace were now lost. People said, "Negotiations can never work. We must go back to fighting."

Both Desmond Tutu and Nelson Mandela had suffered terribly at the hands of the nationalist government. And now one of their fellow leaders had been shot. But they chose to turn back from hatred and bitterness. They pleaded with all South Africans to follow their example. And miraculously, they did. The South African people chose to talk, not fight; to listen and not shoot; to reach out their hands to people of all races. Eleven months later, the first free and fair elections were held, and a truly democratic government was elected. Nelson Mandela became the first President of the new South Africa. Later that year, he and ex-President F.W. de Klerk were awarded the Nobel Peace Prize. There is an alternative to war. A peaceful revolution is possible. South Africa is proof of it.

Helen Brain

The Gift Child

The new toga was scratching Kormi. Mareema had made it for her, especially for her to wear today. It was lovely, she knew, but it made her afraid to move.

"Would you like a drink of water?" asked Obidika. She must be important today. Water was never allowed between meals. No matter how hot the weather was. And it could be hot, here, in the desert.

Obidika had not waited for her reply. Already he was pouring the costly liquid from the large stone jug into a small clay tumbler.

"They're coming," Olib shouted. He rushed through the opening in the tent. His face glistened with sweat.

Kormi was trembling so much she could hardly hold the cup to her lips.

"Drink," said Obidika. Kormi had never heard him sound cross before. But she guessed he was nervous too.

They watched as the hill people came towards them. The women's gowns, so much richer and more colorful than their own, flapped in the wind. The men looked awkward in their long leggings. The horses were slipping on the sand.

"Those are really my people," thought Kormi. "Perhaps even my brothers and sisters are with them."

"Are you ready?" asked Obidika. "Remember, if you hadn't been there they would have attacked by now. They need our water."

The hill people were now just a few yards in front of them. Kormi stared. They looked so strange. Their skin was so pale.

"I must have looked like that once," thought Kormi. She could see her sun-baked arm.

The hill people talked amongst themselves. A tall man nodded to the girl in the dark pink gown.

"Karik-to-kall, Kormi," she said. "Basm ent alake."

Suddenly Kormi remembered. There was another time, when she lived in the shade of leafy trees, and when a woman she called Mother and a man she called Father had looked after her and loved her, and spoken to her with similar words.

She had been very young the last time she used words such as these.

"Who are you?" she asked, using a little awkwardly words from the language she had just heard.

"I am your cousin, Nashreen," said the girl in pink. "Don't you remember me? I was about as big as you are now when you were given."

Kormi looked again at the older girl. Yes! Now she remembered. The brook where they used to swim and splash each other. And making hats to shade against the sun from the leaves of the umbaya tree. And oh, the sweetness of the umbaya fruit.

"We have brought you supplies of umbaya fruits," said Nashreen. "Do you remember the umbaya trees?"

"So, you can't play in the brook now?" said Kormi.

"There is no brook, any more," said Nashreen.

"There hasn't been for many years."

Obidika was watching them. He must have understood the word "brook." He looked uncomfortable. Kormi shifted her weight from one foot to the other. This was what it was all about. And somehow she had to make her cousin understand that the desert people could not give their water away. They had hardly enough for themselves.

"Here, take," said Nashreen. She unclipped a small knife from her belt and took one of the yellow umbayas from the bag on her back. She cut a slice and bit into it. She handed it to Kormi.

Kormi took a bite. Oh yes. This was it! That taste. She had almost forgotten it, like she had almost forgotten her life on the hills. But now it was almost as if she had never left the green slopes.

Nashreen laughed as Kormi enjoyed the fruit. The juice ran down the younger girl's chin. But she didn't care. Just one more bite, she wanted. Then another and another. It was so different from the dried salted meats the desert people ate.

"There are plenty more where those came from," said Nashreen. "Or there will be if we could guarantee a water supply."

Obidika was staring at Kormi.

"Offer him some," whispered Nashreen. She cut another slice and gave it to Kormi. Kormi carried it slowly over to Obidika.

"My people offer you umbaya fruit," she said.

Obidika slowly took a slice of the yellow fruit. He

sniffed it suspiciously and then put it in his mouth. Kormi watched anxiously as he chewed.

"It is good," he murmured at last.

"Tell him there are plenty more of those," cried Nashreen. "Tell him our engineers will help the desert people construct more wells. We won't steal their water. We'll help them find more."

Kormi translated quickly into the language of the people who took care of her.

Nashreen looked at the other hill people. She smiled. They seemed to relax a little. She nodded. They at once set to, unloading the carts and handing over the umbaya fruits to the desert people who had gathered around Obidika's tent.

It was agreed at last. The hill people would send their best engineers and a proportion of all the umbaya fruits which grew each year. The desert people would allow in return as much water as the hill people needed. And if there was not enough for both, then the engineers from both tribes would work together on finding more.

At last, the hill people set off home. Obidika put an arm around Kormi's shoulder.

"You have fulfilled your promise, Gift Child," he said. "There was, after all, no threat."

Kormi smiled to herself. She could still taste the sweet juice of the umbaya. She was glad there would be very many more in the next years.

Gill James

Best Wishes Always

You have wished upon your shooting stars
But I've wished upon the spider
Who has built a web
To catch them as they fall
Downward from the night-time sky,
Falling into morning.

Like silver fish the stars lie caught,
Dream-glittering in dew time
To prove to all
In this war-worn world
Some beauty will survive.

Mark Svendsen

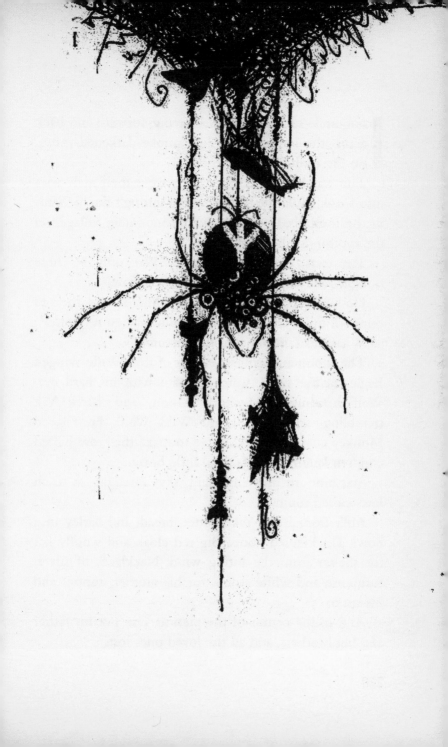

Tam The Eldest

I n a circle sat the women weaving, forward and back across the loom, in the low smoke-darkened room, on the rooftop of the world.

Tam watched them work. They wove their memories into wool, while the invaders stole through the orchards in the foothills, towards the little mountain village, on the rooftop of the world.

Tam was ten. He thought, "War will be here tonight." He thought, "I am the eldest now."

He said "Leave now. Take the children and the old ones. I'll finish the picture and follow when it's done."

What did Tam put into the picture?

The mountain with its crown of mist. Wide-winged Eagle on the wind, watching Tam with his hard eye. Wolf howling at Lantern Moon, and Black Yak trembling when he heard Wild Wolf! Frost-faced Monkey chattering in the tree to make the crow-haired children laugh. Tam's faithful little horse.

Starshine in the midnight sky. Firelight in each low-roofed room.

Milk from Black Yak. Butter, bread, and barley in a bowl. Thick-soled boots. Big red cloak and woolly hat for shelter from the biting wind. Necklaces of silver, turquoise and white stones for his mother, aunties and his sisters.

And in the center of the picture, Tam put his father and big brothers, and all the loved ones lost.

War echoed on the mountainside. Darkness slid along the pass. The fire died, but Tam worked on, finishing their village home under Heaven's starry bowl. He had just begun his boat when he heard the thud of boots!

So from the loom he took the picture, rolled it tight and slung it on his back.

Through the dread night hurried Tam, hearing behind him the boom of war, the shouting and the bullets whine. He turned to look back only once.

The sky was on fire. His village was gone.

Through the darkness hurried Tam, scrambling down the mountainside, clambering on an old rope-bridge across a roaring river. He stopped. He could not move for fear!

Then Tam remembered who was with him.

He heard the crow-haired children cry "HOLD ON!" They cheered his tightrope walk until he reached the other side.

He heard his Father calling "TAM! Take heart" and his brothers shouting "TAM! We're here with you! Everything you need you carry on your back."

And it was.

When Tam was cold, he had the cloak and hat for shelter from the biting wind. When his feet were sore he found the thick-soled boots. Hungry, he had the bowl to feed him. Thirsty, he had milk from Black Yak. Weary, he had his faithful little horse to carry him on her back. Lost, he had Lantern Moon to light the way, and lonely, he had frost-faced Monkey to make him smile.

But the invaders still came after him, down the mountain trail! Tam launched his boat into the river, but it began to sink. Then wide-winged Eagle rode the wind, and carried Tam to land above the border. When a red-eyed demon leaped out of a cave, Wild Wolf chased it far away. When Tam was ambushed, he threw down necklaces of silver, turquoise and white stone. While his attackers squabbled, Tam escaped, over the border at last.

Spread before him was the town.

Its lights and signs and sounds muffled river's rush and Eagle's cry, hid Wolf's howl and Monkey's chatter, dimmed Lantern Moon and Heaven's starry bowl.

So down to the end of the mountain trail came Tam the Eldest, slow as a snail now, carrying his home on his back. From the rooftop of the world, Tam brought his people's memories safely to them.

And he finished his boat.

Caroline Pitcher

The Figure Of Peace

Yes, we know what war is.
We can draw guns, bombs, bodies.

But what does peace look like?

A dove has lent me her white feather to write with.
And I will sing of the silence that echoes after noise,
of the first smile when you see he is alive,
when she knocks on the door again,
when tears run for joy.

I will sing of breaking bread with friends,
of hugging and laughter,
of tucking in bed and waking up with a kiss.

I will sing of the day we turn our faces to the sun and
smile again,
see leaves lifted by a little breeze
and feel our hearts stir like a dove,
lift lighter than air,
and fly us again to the stars.

Wendy Blaxland

Wild Strawberries

We wanted to lay a wreath of heather for Thea. The Dogwood trees were in bloom, their elliptical leaves casting wavy shadows across the trail winding above the city. Blossoms of white burst forth; shut tight for the long years. Trunks blackened and straining out from the hill like a crooked old man reaching for the sun.

And the bees, hibernating more than one winter. Now hours, days after the pacts had been signed, the air hummed. Had some beekeeper secretly fed the bees rationed nectar during the war years? Maybe the bees were smarter than we, understanding how to survive the relentless battles and bombings?

The sun was rising, layering the settling haze. Black, gray, blue. Blue, gray, black. Jez and I climbed the rocky edge of the hill overlooking the battlefields on one side and the city, clinging to the northern wall, on the other. We wanted to lay a wreath of heather for Thea.

The wreath hung over my forearm. Jez chided me, telling me I looked like an old woman with too many shopping bags. But she didn't want to carry it; she had her lucky stick. That was enough.

I shaded my eyes and looked round. Pieces of the castle peeked out of the burnt remains. At our feet, the ground, damp and charred, stuck to our shabby boots. We picked our way through burnt-brambles along the ramparts, our loose-fitting clothes snagging. Up here you are aware that down is easier than you want it to be. It's only a stumble, a tumble of gathering thorny branches and soot all the way back to where the forked trail begins. It's that, or trip one of the many landmines, like Thea.

I sighed and stopped. Jez, her glossy chestnut hair braided round and round her head like a tall crown held with one small twig, tramped on, testing the ground, always testing. I thought for a moment that I reached out and told her to watch her step; but inarticulate, immovable, I said nothing.

She turned and grinned at me, her green eyes laughing. She was a mind reader. A strand of hair loosened, catching the sun. She held up her long stick and shook it, defiant. She used it to test for the hidden mines. Trained to hunt them out. She was a specialist like Thea. But one step too quickly taken... I couldn't stomach the business. I'd stayed in the city with the other kids, master of the sirens and flares.

But Jez had stalked the enemy, unravelling their defenses.

And now she was back.

I hoped she'd stay.

I gazed down at the shattered domes and sniffed the fresh, smokeless air. A city awakening. A city of kids like us. Years of blackened skies and dim memories of another life. One where you didn't scrounge for scraps to eat. One where the snow still fell in the mountains and, melted, ran down to meet you. Not a dry creek

bed. Some of us remembered how it was before. Jez and I were the oldest. Thea would have been, but she was impatient.

"Marco, come!" Jez called. She stood on the far southern side. I hesitated, not sure where to place my feet.

"Follow the trail. It's safe," she said and waved me toward her. "Come!"

I was on hands and knees, crawling up to her.

Jez sat perched atop a loose, leafy, blue-green carpeted knoll. She took the wreath, now, and pulled me up to her. My heart leapt crazy delight, making me dizzy. I captured my breath and held it a moment; prepared myself for the one touch that had kept me wanting to live.

But instead, she held up a single red berry and slipped it into my hungry mouth. "Taste," she said.

And I tasted the valleys below and the skies above. I tasted a thousand flowers. I tasted the lost-but-not-forgotten.

Then she kissed me.

Erzsi Deàk

Alasdair's Lullaby

Go to sleep, my bonnie boy
you're your mammie's pride and joy.
Do not cry
close your eyes
go to sleep, my baby.

There is nothing you should fear
nothing that need cause you tears
while you lie
beside me here.
Go to sleep, my baby.

Time will pass, and you will grow
tall and strong, then you will know –
wars they come
and worlds they go.
Go to sleep, my baby.

Go to sleep, my little one
you are safe and you are warm.
We will shield you
while we can –
go to sleep, my baby.

Anne MacLeod

Dreaming of Peace

Peace
Sat next to us
Spreading her skirt on the earth.
Peace became our mother.

We have prevailed over our past.
All wars have faded away
From our records, epitaphs, and memories.

Necessity for poems
Yearning for peace
Are mere imprints in our books
Like fossils.

How pleasant this feeling of
Universal amity and happiness.

Today, I am late for school
Because of peace.
My mother must have seen me dreaming
But just could not bear
To wake me up.

Ayla Cinaroglu
Translated by David Chou

Where I Live

Where I live the ground is white all through the long
winter and the sun never shines.
We glide over the snow to the ringing of sleigh bells
and the calls of the deer.
High in the sky, waves of light flash through the night
like the sails of ghost ships ploughing through the stars.

Where I live the forest is deep and hot and never still.
We tiptoe over ancient footsteps, silent as air.
Dark is the jungle and full of shadows, but through the
weave of leaves, birds and lizards shine like rainbows –
and high in the treetops bright flowers grow.

Where I live water falls through the mountains like
fountains of jewels.
We take our sheep up steep paths, the sky so close
that we walk through clouds.
When we look down on the green valleys they seem
as far away as dreams.

Where I live the land is red and orange, gold and brown.
We climb hills that rise like towers, and canyons carved
from stone beneath an endless sky.
When night falls coyotes call to the moon and we sleep
in a field of stars.

Where I live palm trees dance in the wind, and the sky
is smudged with clouds of birds.
Beneath the surface of the blue-green sea is
a kaleidoscope of color.
The rice paddies are luminous on still afternoons,
and we catch dragonflies as though fishing in air.

Where I live the sky is red and orange at dusk when
the elephants come to the river to bathe.
The monkeys chatter in the trees, but we move quietly over
the water in our small boats, quick to reach the shore before
the water lilies snap shut and night descends.

Where I live the water of the lake lies in stripes
of yellow, green, red, black and brown.
We gather bark and berries in the woods, walking
carefully through the webs that span the trees like lace.
At night we sit in moonshine and tell stories that
hold us through time.

Where I live stars shine in the sea as well as in the sky.
Fish fly through the air, and birds swim in the water.
We ride on the waves, singing the songs of the wind.

Where I live the green islands twist through the ocean
like snakes, and smoke rises from the mountain tops.
On gentle days we ride boats with bright sails and chimes
made of shells, and swim with the dolphins far from
the shore.

Where I live it snows flowers in the springtime
and rains fire in the autumn.
In the winter we slide beneath trees that might have
been carved from ice.
In the summer we chase the tiny lights that flicker
in the shadows of the night.

Where I live there are no rivers and no lakes, no forests,
no mountain and no fields.
We race our ponies over seas of sand, and move with
the sun, the sky all around us, knowing our place by
watching the stars.

Where we live is on the planet Earth.

Dyan Sheldon

Index of Titles

Index of Contributors

Index of Artists

Acknowledgements

The editors and publisher would like to thank: Oxford University Press for Rachel Anderson's *Lost and Found*, modified from *Warlands*, first published in 2000; Orchard Books for Laurence Anholt's characters from *Eco-Wolf and the Three Pigs*, one of the Seriously Silly Stories first published in 1999; Brenda Skinner's account from *Waiting for the All Clear* by Ben Wicks, first published by Bloomsbury in 1990 for providing the inspiration for Bernard Ashley's *Out Shopping*; Orion Books, Aurthur A. Levine Books and Scholastic Press for *Jihad*, taken from *King of the Middle March*, the third part of Kevin Crossley-Holland's *Arthur* trilogy first published in October 2003; Pennine Pens for Simon Fletcher's *Gulf*, taken from *Email from the Provinces*, first published in 2000; Sabina Horvat for *Heartmines*, illustrated by Martin Olsson, which was first published on-line in 2002 at www.landmines.org.uk by Adopt-A-Minefield (UK) and Storycircus Ltd; Anderson Press for the extract of Julia Jarman's *The Peace Weavers*, to be published shortly; Egmont Children's Books for Susie Jenkin-Pearce's *Family Photo*, '45 from *Dove On The Roof: A Collection of Poems about Peace*, edited by Jennifer Curry, first published in 1992; CICADA for Anne Levine's *Yield! Narrow Passage Ahead*, a version of which was published in the January 2003 issue of their magazine; Bloodaxe Books for Adrian Mitchell's *On the Beach at Cambridge* from *Heart on the Left: Poems 1953-1984*, first published in 1997; HarperCollins Childrens Books for Michael Morpurgo's *For Carlos: A Letter From Your Father*, from *Kids' Night In*, published in 2003, Faber & Faber for Judith Nicholls' *Evolution*, from *Dragonsfire*, first published in 1990; St. Martin's Press for Jane Yolen's *The Singer and the Song*, taken from *Sister Emily's Lightship and Other Stories*, first published in 2001; and Stephen Raw for providing the lettering of the title on the front cover.

Photographic Acknowledgements

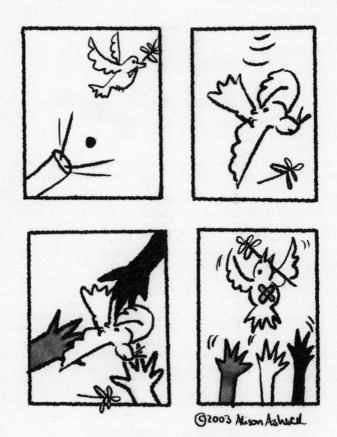

©2003 Alison Ashwell